Love on the Rocks

Cobble Cove Mystery #4

By Debbie De Louise

Solstice Publishing - http://www.solsticeempire.com/

To my love, my husband Anthony.

Prologue

"Alicia, come with me to the Reference Desk. Nancy left a few more decorations there this morning, and maybe we can find some room for them down here. Otherwise, you can run them up to her."

Alicia followed Sheila back to the desk, admiring the paper hearts and flowers hanging from the library ceiling and the red streamers that lay across the stacks. Sheila rifled through some of the additional decorations that were piled next to the reference PC. She reminded Alicia of a hen tending her chickens. "Gilly and Ramsay will be so surprised."

Alicia agreed. The idea for a combination wedding and Valentine's Day party was hatched up by Sheila, and it was a great thought. The rest of the staff was busy upstairs arranging more decorations and putting out all the homecooked dishes they'd prepared along with the red, pink, and white sheet cake that would be served for dessert.

"What's this?" Sheila paused in her tossing of decorations atop the desk.

Alicia came over to see what had grabbed the director's attention. A velvet heart shaped box sat by one of the computer stations. As Alicia came closer, she could see a post-it attached to it with the words, "To Sheila from your secret admirer."

Sheila smiled. "That Ryan. He knows I have a sweet tooth and am particularly fond of chocolates." She opened the lid. "My favorites. I know I should wait for the party, but these are just too appealing."

Alicia watched as Sheila took a piece and bit into it. Only a few seconds after she swallowed, her smile faded. She began to choke and clutched her throat.

"Sheila, are you okay?" Alicia tried to remember how to do the Heimlich maneuver, but Sheila had already passed out on the floor. "Help!" she called, racing to the stairs. The romantic music playing above drowned out her voice. Just as she grabbed her cell phone to dial 911, Ryan Anderson walked through the door, a huge bouquet of roses in his arms. He stopped short, seeing Sheila on the ground. "What happened? Oh my God!"

"I'm dialing 911 right now," Alicia said. "She ate one of your chocolates and then passed out. I'm not sure if she choked on a piece."

"My chocolates? I didn't get her any chocolates. I was bringing her these flowers." He dropped them on the desk and then knelt, administering CPR to Sheila's unmoving body.

Chapter One
A Week Earlier

It was a sunny yet cold February day in the small town of Cobble Cove. Alicia McKinney, standing by the library windows looking out at the icy flakes drifting down, remarked to Sheila, the library's director, "I still can't believe Gilly eloped with Ramsay."

Sheila tossed back her red hair, constrained by a white headband. "At their age, they probably wanted something small, Alicia. That doesn't stop us from holding a party for them when they return from their honeymoon."

"Great idea. Maybe I can arrange something with Edith and Rose at the inn. You know how good Edith is at party planning, but she'll have to work quick. They'll be back from Hawaii tomorrow."

"I'd be happy to offer the library's meeting room for the event if they need more space."

Alicia considered. She recalled how she and John had used the meeting room for the release party for their last mystery five months ago. They were currently hard at work on the third book of the series with a new editor, Mary Lou, the twin sister of the woman who was murdered last September and whose body was found in the library's mystery stacks. The memory caused a shudder to run up her spine.

"I'll check with Edith. Thanks, Sheila."

Sheila smiled and turned to make her way back to the reference desk. In the last few weeks, Alicia had noticed a difference in her boss. There was a blush to her cheeks and a lightness in her step. If Alicia didn't know better, she'd think Sheila was seeing someone, but she'd been a widow for over thirty years. The only man she'd seemed interested in was Alicia's husband John and that was only as a friend.

"Sheila, can I ask you something?" She brought the director's attention back.

"Of course, Alicia."

She took a deep breath. "Are you, uh, do you have a . . ."

Sheila smiled, her green eyes catlike slits. Then in a low voice she replied, "I'm surprised you didn't ask me sooner. Yes, I have an admirer. It's been a long time since I entertained the idea of a suiter. But life's too short, and Ryan is such a gentleman."

"Ryan? You don't mean . . ."

Sheila nodded, tucking a loose strand of hair back under the band with a hand laden with rings. "Yes, I do. Professor Ryan Anderson."

Alicia tried not to display her shock. No wonder Sheila had been spending so much time with the whitehaired English professor from California. She'd insisted on acting as his own personal research assistant when he'd started coming to the library for help a few weeks ago.

"Don't look so surprised, Alicia. If your best friend could marry again after her first husband cheated on her and your father-in-law, in his eighties, has found romance with another senior, why do you think it would be so difficult for me to start dating again?"

Alicia swallowed the lump that had formed in her throat. "I didn't mean that, Sheila. You're an attractive woman. I just thought . . ." She fumbled for the words. "I was under the impression you were still grieving for your husband."

Sheila let out a short laugh. "Alicia, he's been dead for so long. Of course, I remember him fondly. I miss him. I wish he'd been around to see my daughter and our grandchildren, but I know he would approve of my seeing another man. The reason I haven't until now is because no one has interested me. Ryan is different. He's a lot like Tom. He reminds me of him, but it's more than that." Her green eyes widened as she tried to describe her feelings. "I enjoy talking with him. He's a prolific reader, and a very intelligent man. Did you know he graduated from Harvard?"

"No. I really don't know much about him, Sheila. He doesn't mingle much with the staff."

She laughed lightly again. "I guess I take up too much of his time and his research, of course."

"I don't mean to pry, Sheila, but has he reciprocated your interest? I mean, have you two actually gone out somewhere outside the library?"

Sheila lowered her eyes as if to study a spot on the floor. "He hasn't asked me anywhere yet, but I'm planning to invite him over for dinner one night."

Alicia hesitated in voicing her opinion on this matter, but Sheila was a friend to her as well as a boss. "Do you think that's a good idea? I may be old-fashioned, but shouldn't you wait until he asks you out?"

Sheila shrugged. "Perhaps I need to wait a little longer. Valentine's Day is next Friday. I have a feeling he's planning something for me."

"Are you sure he's available? Do you know if he's married or seeing someone?"

"There's no band on his wedding finger."

"That doesn't always mean anything." Alicia recalled how her first husband never wore his ring, although John wore his dead wife's ring for years after she passed away.

"Trust me, Alicia. I know when a man is taken. Ryan is too wrapped up in his work to spend much time dating, and I know he lives alone because I've called him several times. A woman never answers the phone."

Alicia didn't know how to respond. She hoped Sheila was right, or she was in for a big letdown.

As Sheila went back to the desk to join Donald who was waiting to be relieved for his lunch break, Alicia saw John pushing the twins in their double stroller toward the library's entrance. She noticed he'd pulled both stroller canopies over their heads to protect them from the snow, but he'd left his coat hood down, and bits of white clung to his dark hair. She went to greet him by the turnstiles.

"What a surprise, John. What brings you here with Carol and Johnny?"

He grinned, displaying the dimple in his left cheek she found so attractive. "Could be I want to check out a book. I do have a library card, you know."

She laughed. "I think you and the kids just miss me." As soon as they were through the turnstile, she lowered the canopies and peeked at her toddlers. She couldn't believe that in only three months, they would be two years old. John had done well in dressing them up in heavy clothes. Despite the sunshine, temperatures were at the freezing point. She unlatched Carol and removed her pink knit cap, allowing her blonde curls to escape. Neither she nor John were blondes, but Carol took after her aunt Pamela and cousins Cynthia and Caroline. Johnny, whom John unbuckled after he parked the stroller to the side of the library's front door, took after his father in dark good looks and quiet demeanor. Carol was already gibbering as the staff gathered round to admire the twins whom they practically considered part of the family.

"They're getting so big," Sheila commented.

After closing out his Facebook page, Donald came around the desk to take a better look at the twins. Johnny reached out as Donald bent down and tugged on his heart-covered tie. "Ouch," Donald exclaimed, pulling away. "Be careful with that, young man. It was a gift from Roger for last year's Valentine's Day. I hope he gets me another one with Cupids or something this year."

Alicia laughed. Donald collected the gaudiest ties. "I think the colors attracted him. He loves bright things."

"What about Carol? What is she gabbing about?"

Alicia shook her head. "Who knows? She talks pretty much non-stop when she's awake. I have no idea where she gets that from. I was a very quiet child, and John's not a talker either. We're both writers, so we tend to be introverts."

"Could be she gets it from Mac," Donald pointed out. "When he comes to the library to pick up the books he repairs at home, he doesn't stop chatting with me. When I don't respond, he starts talking to Fido who usually accompanies him."

"As long as Fido doesn't answer him," John said. "By the way, where is Sneaky?"

"I think he's in the Children's Room with Laura and Jean, napping in that sunny bay window. Let's take a walk over there. I'm sure they'll be dying to see the kids."

"No need. We're right here, Alicia." Jean and Laura strode over from the archway that connected the Children's Room from the Adult Reference area. Jean, the part-time librarian, was working extra hours to help Laura in the Children's Room since Gilly was away on her honeymoon. She was also helping at the reference desk, when needed, since Vera had retired at the end of December. She took Carol from her co-worker's arms and began conversing with her. Laura, the young full-time Children's Librarian, joined in with a few of her own words that Carol quickly mimicked.

"Will you look at that?" John said. "You have two toddler translators on staff."

Alicia punched him lightly in the arm, making sure not to hit Johnny's dangling baby shoes. Jean said, "My son Jeremy talked at a very young age, too. I'm sure your being a librarian and you and John reading to them each night really helped their language skills."

Laura added, "I've always found it easy to talk to babies and animals." Alicia recalled how the pretty blonde, along with her new boyfriend, Matt, had helped find Sneaky after he disappeared the night that her and John's editor was murdered. Like Laura, Matt was a true animal lover and volunteered at the same rescue shelter that she did.

As Jean and Laura gabbed with Carol, Sneaky came exploring on brown padded paws to see what all the fuss was about. Johnny reached out to pet the Siamese.

"Be careful. That cat has a bite," Donald teased. Alicia knew he had a soft spot for Sneaky but wouldn't admit to it. She also knew that Sneaky was gentle and would never harm one of the twins. He even stayed with them occasionally at their house when the library was closed. When it was open, he wandered around the Children's Room, sometimes participating in story times and taking advantage of the scraps left in the break room which was a cat flap away from the room where his litter box, cat tree, and other toys were stored.

"Excuse me, people. I know the twins are adorable, but you all must get back to work," Sheila said, returning to the desk. She glanced over at Alicia. "You can take your break now, Alicia, and spend a few minutes with your family."

"Thanks, Sheila."

As Jean reluctantly handed Carol back to her mother, she took Alicia aside and asked, "Is something going on with Sheila?"

Alicia wasn't sure she should say anything, but Sheila hadn't vowed her to secrecy. "We'll talk about it later, Jean."

"What about me?" Laura whispered.

"Both of you. I promise."

Jean shook back her dark hair and walked back to the Children's Room. Laura scooped up Sneaky, murmuring to him that she was returning him to his window seat, so he could resume his nap.

John and Alicia went upstairs to the staff break room for some privacy. They put Johnny and Carol down and let them walk up next to them, each holding a tiny hand.

"They're doing great," Alicia commented. "Still a bit wobbly on their feet, but faster."

"Spoken like a proud mother."

"Was there something you wanted to see me about today, John? You don't often come to the library when I'm working."

"But my heart's with you wherever I am."

She smiled. "Romantic today. What's up? Do you need a favor?"

His smile widened. "Is that what you think? That I'm leading up to asking for something?"

They were at the door of the break room.

"Let's sit down, John. I don't see anyone else up here." She took a seat across from him and sat Carol on her lap. Her daughter had quieted down since her lengthy chat with Jean and Laura. "No, I don't think you want something, but I'm curious. Why did you bring the kids out in the cold? I'm only here a few more hours. It could've waited until I got home."

John, following her example, propped Johnny on his knee. "If you must know, Ali. I was a little bored and wanted to get some fresh air. I'm sure it did the kids good, too. It's hard being in the house all the time in winter. But there is something else . . ."

"Oh? Spill it, Mr. McKinney."

His chuckle echoed through the empty room. "You know that a special holiday is coming up next week, right?"

She pretended ignorance. "Holiday? In February? Groundhog's Day already passed."

"You know I'm talking about Valentine's Day, Mrs. McKinney."

"Ah. Yes, how could I forget? What about it, John?"

"I was thinking we need a date night. We haven't had one since we lost our babysitter."

Alicia was all too aware that Kim's taking a job at the paper in Carlsville had left a big gap in their lives. Not only didn't they have a babysitter, but John was out an intern on the newspaper. Luckily, Andy, his other intern, had taken on most of that work, but it was probably only a matter of time before he joined his girlfriend on her paper. Then John would need to find a way to balance working on their mystery novels with publishing the *Cobble Cove Courier*, the town's newspaper, each week. The babies wouldn't be starting pre-school for another year, so that would be an issue that Alicia, still working at the library and co-authoring their mystery series, would also have to deal with.

"I'd definitely be up for a date night John, but remember that Gilly and Ramsay return from their honeymoon tomorrow, and we're planning a party for them."

"We are?" He raised an eyebrow.

"Well, Sheila was discussing one with me. It would be a combination wedding and Valentine's Day party here in the library if there's not enough room in the inn."

"Might be fun, but I still want some time alone with my wife. Any idea of when we can arrange that? We could ask Mac and Betty to watch the babies."

Alicia knew her father-in-law and his girlfriend would be thrilled to babysit the twins, but they would most likely be going out to dinner to celebrate their own romantic holiday. "Let me check with Betty and see when they're available. We don't have to go on Friday when the whole world is celebrating."

He grinned. "If it was up to me, we'd be celebrating every night. But, sure, pick a night, pick a place. I don't care where or when as long as we're together."

"That certainly sounds romantic," A voice came from behind Alicia. She spun around to see Nancy Haines, the PR Director, enter the break room. She was dressed in a smart tailored peacock blue suit decorated with a scarf patterned in soft-colored paisley accents.

"Hi, Nancy," Alicia greeted her. "Are you on break?"

"About to be, but I'll come back later if that's more convenient. I'm sorry I interrupted you."

"No worries," John said. "I need to get these little guys back home, anyway. They look like they're ready for their nap." Johnny's head had slumped down against John's chest, and his eyes were barely open, hooded by his long lashes. Carol also seemed sleepy as she nestled against Alicia's sweater.

"They're beautiful." Nancy said. "Like little angels."

"You haven't seen them when they're wide awake."

"Oh, you don't have to tell me that, John. Before I decided to go into PR work, I wanted to be a teacher. I student taught a kindergarten class, and although the kids were older than your toddlers, they were certainly a handful."

Alicia hadn't known this part of Nancy's history. "Is that why you went into PR instead?"

"No. I enjoyed teaching, but I met my husband at that time. He convinced me to take on more of a challenge."

"More challenging than teaching kindergarten?" John pulled up Johnny who, having fallen asleep, was slipping off his knee.

"I sometimes regret the advice my ex gave me, but maybe it turned out for the best. I love PR work."

"You've never talked about children," Alicia said. "I hope I'm not prying by asking if you ever had any?"

Nancy's dark eyes widened. "No, Alicia. I wasn't married long, so it was just as well we hadn't started a family. But on a more interesting topic, before you leave, I have something I want to run by you. I'd like John's opinion, too."

"Sure." It was common for Nancy to try out ideas for library promotions with Alicia as well as Sheila. Even though she'd been the PR director since that summer, she still wasn't totally comfortable in the position.

"Thanks. What do you two think of our holding a Valentine Party here in the library on Friday? We could tie it in with one of those mystery book things—Date with a Book where the librarians select books of various genres, wrap them up in theme paper with hearts and cupids and put them on a hand truck by the circulation desk for people to check out. It's a great way for people to discover different authors and writing styles. We could have some refreshments upstairs and a heart-shaped cake for the occasion. I'm sure Duncan would be happy to supply some hero sandwiches, and Claire has already started creating some beautiful Valentine cakes."

"I'm in for the food," John said.

Alicia tapped him. "John's always in for the food. I like the idea, but I would like to suggest one tiny change."

Nancy leaned forward as if to hear better. Even the twins seemed to perk up and show some interest. Carol began to babble, and Johnny started playing with John's shirt buttons.

"I'd like to propose that we combine the library party with the party Sheila wants to give Gilly and Ramsay when they return from their honeymoon. Do you think that would work?"

Nancy considered. "It might be tricky, although most of the regular patrons know Gilly because she works here part-time as a clerk, and, of course, they know the sheriff. Maybe we could hold the patron party during work hours and Gilly and Ron's party after we close on Valentine's Day. That way, all the decorations and stuff would be up, and we would just need to order additional food."

"One question," John said. "If you're thinking of holding the party on Friday, would you have a problem getting people to attend if they have plans for the holiday? I know I'd like to take the wife out for dinner that night."

"John, we already said we'll plan a different day for our date night. I think attending Gilly and Ramsay's party right here in the library would be a great way to spend Valentine's Day. If people have plans, they don't need to stay for more than an hour or two."

"Makes sense," John agreed.

Nancy's face lit up. "Wonderful! I'll speak with Sheila today and start the ball rolling. Thanks, guys."

Chapter Two

After John took the babies home and Alicia went back to work, Sheila joined her at the desk. "Nancy filled me in on your idea to combine Gilly and Ron's party with a library Valentine's Day party. I love it. Can you help select the Blind Date with a Book choices?"

Alicia never saw Sheila so enthused. "Sure. I'll try to mix up the genres and add some debut authors as well as popular ones."

"Excellent." Sheila's smile widened as she gazed across toward the library's entrance. Professor Anderson was entering. He smiled and waved at them. His usual tweed suit was impeccably tailored, and his thick white hair had no loose strands even though Alicia could hear the wind outside whistling through the trees. She wondered if he used hairspray or if it was a natural-looking hairpiece. He carried a black and white marbled composition book that Alicia recalled using as a child in school.

"Good day, ladies," he said approaching the desk. "I must say this library has the most beautiful librarians."

Sheila's face reddened almost to the shade of her hair, while Donald, passing by with a book truck, snickered. "I've never been called beautiful. Thank you, Professor."

"There's beauty in everyone." Ryan turned to Sheila. "May we get to work, my dear? I hear the English poets calling—Tennyson, Blake, Woodsworth, Keats, and their contemporaries. They're waiting for us. Oh, I almost forgot your poem for today."

Alicia saw Donald roll his eyes when the professor looked away.

Ryan reached across the desk, took Sheila's hand in his, and recited:

She walks in beauty, like the night
Of cloudless climes and starry skies;
And all that's best of dark and bright
Meet in her aspect and her eyes;
Thus mellowed to that tender light
Which heaven to gaudy day denies.

Sheila, still holding Ryan's hand, floated toward him, her boots gliding noiselessly across the library tiles as she joined him. While he wasn't a tall man, she looked up at him from the two inches that separated their heads.

"I love that poem," she said. "You know Lord Byron is one of my favorite poets."

"Mine, as well. Come, let's adjourn to the book room to begin our studies."

"Later. I brought some books up to my office. Can we start there first?"

Alicia caught the wink behind the professor's glasses. "Even better." The two walked side by side to the stairs.

"I think I'm going to be sick," Donald commented as he brought a book truck behind the reference desk. "I don't remember ever being that googly-eyed over Roger even when we first met. I don't think you acted that way over John, either."

"You can't compare me and John, Donald. I was just getting over my husband's death, and John was still grieving for his wife."

"Still. Sheila is no starry-eyed teenager."

"You should be happy for her."

Donald opened the library system's catalog on his PC to start checking the circulation statistics for the books on his cart that might be eligible for discard. Alicia knew he'd open another tab in the browser to read Facebook.

"I don't know why he's here in Cobble Cove to begin with. Isn't he better off at an academic library? New Paltz has a good one."

"He's here because he knows Sheila's family. Her son-in-law works at his college in California, and Sheila's daughter just got a part-time job in the library there."

"But how can our measly collection compare with larger libraries? Even if he's a friend of the family, isn't he looking for the latest material for his research?"

"Not necessarily, Donald. I think he wants the best researcher. Sheila is top notch. You know that."

Donald looked unconvinced. As Alicia expected, he opened his Facebook page and turned back to the computer. "I think he just wants to get in her pants. Her daughter must've shown him her photo. Even though I'm not into women, I can tell she's attractive for a woman her age."

Alicia laughed. "I'm sure there are lots of beautiful women her age in California."

"Then Professor Anderson must be after something else." He typed in his status, "weeding library books," indicated he was feeling bored, posted it, and then turned to Alicia. "I wonder what it is."

***

While Donald went back to his Facebook notices and Alicia busied herself preparing computer passes, Mrs. Rhonda Kleisman bounded through the door carrying a stack of book returns and plopped them down on the counter in front of Alicia. Huffing as she caught her breath, she said, "I was going to drop these in the book drop, but I want to make sure they're checked in properly. Last time, I was charged for a late book that I know I placed on time in the drop."

Alicia knew that wasn't true. The drop was emptied regularly, and Rhonda's book was deposited a week late.

Donald paused in typing a comment on Facebook and whispered, "If it isn't Clydesdale the horse lady."

Alicia tried to hide her grin at Donald's nickname for the rotund patron as she began running the woman's books under the scanner to check them in. She stopped when she came to one that emitted a decaying odor. She opened the cover. There were greasy stains that looked like butter, bits of flour, and what looked like cake batter throughout its pages. This wasn't the first time that she'd returned a damaged book to the library.

"Excuse me, Mrs. Kleisman, but there's some food in this book."

Rhonda's small eyes narrowed. She mimicked surprise. "Food? I don't eat when I read. That must've been left by another patron. Disgusting!"

"I'm afraid that can't be the case, Mrs. Kleisman. We check all our books when they're returned. If any are in poor condition, we either note it so the next patron checking it out won't be charged or we contact the last person on the record and ask them to pay for a replacement."

"What are you saying? Are you accusing me of messing up that book?" Her voice began to rise.

Donald, seeing Alicia's discomfort, came to assist her. "That's exactly what my co-worker is saying, ma'am. You will be charged for the cost of that copy."

Kleisman's nostrils flared, not unlike the horse Donald nicknamed her for. "I want to speak with your superior," she demanded.

Alicia was thankful the library wasn't busy at that point, so no patrons were gathering in a line behind Rhonda. "Our director is in a meeting right now," she explained quietly, knowing that Sheila wouldn't be happy to be disturbed while in Ryan's company.

"Isn't that convenient?" Rhonda's small black eyes enlarged into angry dark bullets. "I don't care if she's meeting with the Pope. I demand to see her."

Alicia glanced at Donald, who shook his head.

"Go, Alicia. Sheila would want you to let her know about this."

Alicia headed upstairs. At the director's office, she hesitated and then knocked gently on the closed door, wondering why it wasn't open. "Sheila," she called when there was no immediate reply. "Sorry to interrupt, but there's a problem downstairs."

After another two minutes, Sheila opened the door. A few strands of her fiery hair were loose and hanging over her headband. Her face was flushed. Behind her, Ryan sat at her desk, a few books open in front of him, looking composed and studious. Alicia knew that Sheila never allowed anyone to sit at her desk.

"Give me a moment. I'll be right down. Excuse me, Ryan," she called back to him.

"No worries, dear. I'll just keep working where we left off."

At those words, Sheila's blush deepened, leaving Alicia to wonder where exactly they'd left off.

***

Alicia filled in Sheila on the way downstairs. The redness of the director's face deepened, this time in anger. "Mrs. Kleisman again? I should ban her from the library."

Back at the desk, Donald was arguing with the irate patron while a long line of people had formed behind her. When Donald saw help had arrived, he sighed in relief.

"Mrs. Kleisman," Sheila said, keeping her voice firm but pasting a smile on her face. "Please come with me, and we can talk."

Donald pushed the woman's books to the other side of the desk while he waved the next patron forward. Alicia joined him as the two women walked away. She wondered where they were going because Sheila's office was currently occupied.

After the crowd was diminished, Alicia excused herself. She hadn't seen Mrs. Kleisman leave the library, and she wondered if Sheila was still talking with her. She walked in the direction the director had taken. They had recently opened a small café in the library for patrons to purchase vending machine snacks, soups, and drinks. The café also featured small tables and, like the rest of the library, allowed free Wi-Fi access. In addition, some outlets were available for charging devices or plugging in laptops. Glancing into the café, Alicia saw it was empty except for Sheila and Mrs. Kleisman who were seated across from one another, each with a cup of coffee. She didn't want to disturb them so stood outside behind the door where she was still able to hear their discussion.

"I can't keep repeating myself, Mrs. Kleisman. You are responsible for the damage to that book. You can pay us by check, cash, or replacement copy. Amazon sometimes sells books at a lower price than the library's discount from Baker and Taylor."

"I don't believe this." Kleisman raised her voice. "I'm a taxpayer. I've lived in this community for thirty years. If Mr. McKinney was still director, he would never ask me to pay a cent."

Alicia knew that probably was true. Mac, despite his reverence for keeping books intact, was a man who shied away from confrontations.

"Well, I'm the current director now and if you don't respect the library's policies, then I will have to take your name before the Board to consider banning you from this building."

"How dare you?" Alicia heard the shuffle of a chair as Mrs. Kleisman stood up. There was the sound of a splash and a cry of pain. Alicia ran into the room as Mrs.

Kleisman was bolting from it, missing her by inches. Sheila stood there covered in coffee. Her lovely suit was dripping and stained.

"Oh, no. Sheila, are you okay?" She grabbed some napkins to try to soak up the mess.

"I'm not burned, but my clothes... Call Gerry quick."

After the murder in September, Sheila had installed several communication devices in the building that connected with the security guard's walkie talkie. Alicia ran to the one on the café's wall and pressed the button. After a crackle of sound, she said, "Gerry. Mrs. Kleisman just threw coffee on Sheila. Don't let her leave the building." Gerry had dealt several times with her in the past. Wherever she went, she always left a mess behind her.

"I need to change and take this to a cleaner," Sheila said. "Can you do me a favor, Alicia? Please go up to my office and let Ryan know I'll be back later. You don't need to tell him about this. Just say I had to check on a few things at my house. If he can't wait, he can call me, and we'll reschedule."

"Sure. Don't worry, Sheila. What are you going to do about Mrs. Kleisman?"

Sheila's green eyes blazed. "I should have her arrested, but I think banning her from the library is just punishment. That woman is not only a pig, but she's dangerous. Considering her actions, I don't even need the Board's permission."

As she and Alicia left the café, they saw Gerry detaining Mrs. Kleisman. "Let me go, or I'll report you!" she yelled.

Patrons watched as Sheila—wet, stained, and smelling of coffee—approached her. "You are no longer welcome in this library, Mrs. Kleisman. If you attempt to enter, I will have you arrested. Is that clear?"

The woman stopped struggling and stared into Sheila's face. "Very well. You can take your library and shove it where the sun doesn't shine. But don't expect me or my family to vote for the budget this year."

"Understood. Have a wonderful day, Mrs. Kleisman."

Alicia watched as the guard nearly tossed the woman out the door. He turned back to them. "Good riddance. That lady is a menace. So sorry about your suit, Ms. Whitehead."

"Thank you, Gerry. I'm going home to change. If she returns or there are any problems, Alicia, call me right away."

Alicia nodded and went back to the reference desk, where Donald murmured, "It's about time they banned her. I'm glad she didn't throw any food on my clothes." He tugged on his tie as if to protect it.

After Sheila left and the patron's whispers died down, Alicia followed Sheila's instructions and went upstairs to speak with Ryan. As she approached the director's office, she noticed the door was closed. She thought Sheila had left it open when she'd gone downstairs, but maybe she was mistaken. She'd been nervous when she'd had to interrupt Sheila and the professor.

Alicia didn't know why she acted the way she did in the next few moments. It went against all her beliefs about privacy, but instead of knocking or calling out to Ryan, she placed her hand on the knob and gently pushed open the door.

She expected surprise, even anger to greet her from the man who stood there. She didn't expect him to be sitting with his back to her looking through Sheila's desk drawer files.

Chapter Three

Alicia stood there, mouth agape, staring at the professor. When she finally found her voice, she said, "Ryan, what are you doing?"

She expected him to jump, flinch, or show some indication of surprise. Instead, he turned around, a smile on his face. "Hello, Alicia. I didn't hear you knock. I was just checking some of the notes Sheila and I were working on before she was called away. Is everything alright? Has she been delayed? I don't mind waiting. I know how much in demand her time is, and I respect the amount she allots me."

"That's right. Sheila had to go home for a few minutes, but she told me to ask you to stay if you could. She'll be back soon."

"Wonderful!" He closed the desk drawer, but Alicia noted he didn't take out any of the papers he and Sheila were working on. Either he hadn't found them, or he was lying about what he was searching for in the director's files.

Alicia hated being suspicious, but being a librarian, it was her nature to question things and look for their answers. Having been involved in three mysteries since she came to Cobble Cove made her even warier of a person's unusual behavior.

"I guess you need to return to the reference desk," Ryan said. She imagined he might be trying to get rid of her, so he could continue canvassing Sheila's office. She tried to rein in her overactive imagination. He and Sheila were collaborating on a project. She'd given him permission to work at her desk. There was nothing strange about that.

"Yes. Would you like me to bring you anything while you wait? Coffee? Tea?"

"No. I'm fine. Thank you. Sheila and I already had some tea." He indicated the two empty mugs on the desk.

Alicia nodded and walked out into the hall. She made sure to leave the door open behind her.

***

The rest of the day was uneventful. Sheila returned within the hour and thanked Alicia for letting Ryan know she had to go home but not telling him what happened with the irate patron. She spent the rest of the morning in her office. Alicia was tempted to mention that she'd found the professor looking through her files, but she'd never been a rat, and she knew Sheila would just confirm the fact that she was sharing research with Ryan for his book.

Reference was slow, and she was thankful the patrons who visited the desk were pleasant. Donald had pushed aside the damaged books Mrs. Kleisman had dumped there. "Those really should be brought to Circulation," Alicia said.

Donald made a face. "I'm not touching them, but you can do the honors." He handed her a pair of vinyl gloves the librarians used when handling soiled material.

Alicia gingerly picked up the books. She noticed they were dessert cookbooks and diet books, a strange mix, but the woman who had checked them out was even stranger.

At the circ desk, she instructed Bonnie to remove their records from the computer and discard them. It was unlikely the library would recoup a cent from Mrs. Kleisman.

"Ick," Bonnie exclaimed as Alicia placed the books on the counter. She gazed at them through the oval lenses of her horn-rimmed glasses and pushed back her cocoa bangs. "These are that crazy lady's books, right? The one who threw coffee on Sheila?"

"Yep. Hopefully, we won't be seeing her again."

Bonnie took the gloves Alicia had removed and put them on. Flipping to the back page of the chocolate-making book, she said, "These are going in the trash as soon as I scan their barcodes."

Alicia smiled. "Sounds like a plan. Thanks, Bonnie."

***

That night, at the dinner table, Alicia recounted the story to John and the babies as he cut up slices of chicken for Carol and Johnny. She left nothing out, including her catching Professor Anderson searching for alleged book notes in Sheila's desk.

"Whoa." John placed a few chicken chunks on Johnny's high chair plate next to the chopped up green beans and mashed potatoes. Then he speared a chunk and told the toddler, "The train is coming down the tracks." Johnny opened his mouth, took a bite off the fork, and John smiled. "Good boy. Now Choo Choo." Johnny chomped down on the food, his chubby cheeks expanding, so that the dimple that matched his dad's was obvious.

Alicia normally wouldn't be happy about her conversation being interrupted, but she loved to watch John feed their children. Next was Carol, and John repeated the procedure, moving his chair next to his daughter. Carol wasn't as compliant as her brother. At first, she kept her lips tightly pursed, which was uncommon for the girl who loved to talk. John tried to persuade her with, "Yummy chicken, Carol. Take a bite."

"No twain," she said.

John laughed. "What about a plane? Wheee," he mimicked flying with his arms. "Or a car? Vroom Vroom."

Alicia found the sight of John holding the fork and making sounds and gestures funny. It was obvious Carol was smarter than that and was already wise to John's tactics. When John waved the baby fork a second time, she took it in her tiny hand, bit off the chicken, chewed, and swallowed. She ended by licking her lips with her tongue, handing the fork back to John, and saying, "More, Daddy, more."

Alicia couldn't contain herself. "Daddy, I think you've been bested by a two-year-old."

"Fine," John said, pretending to be insulted. "I'll finish feeding my son. You deal with your daughter, Mommy." He took Carol's plate, filled it with half the chicken he'd cut and placed it in front of Alicia. Then he moved back to Johnny and started spearing chicken and making train noises.

Alicia laughed out loud. She knew Johnny also no longer needed the train narrative to eat, but he was making the most of his father's attention. She also knew that she'd have to wait to continue their talk after the kids were in bed.

Carol and Johnny had recently moved from their cribs to twin beds but were still sharing the nursery. Alicia planned to wait until they started school before moving one of them into the guest room across the hall.

As their normal bedtime routine, John and Alicia took turns reading the kids stories from library books or from their own collection of picture books. When both had fallen asleep, Carol with her thumb in her mouth, a habit Alicia was still trying to break her of and John with his stuffed teddy by his side, John switched off the lights, and he and Alicia walked together next door to their bedroom.

"I know you're just busting to hear what I have to say about your experience at the library," John said after he'd brushed his teeth and changed. Alicia had already used the bathroom and was indeed anxious to finish their discussion.

It was still early, but they'd gotten into the habit of going to bed after their children, so they could write on their laptops or work together on a storyline to their next book. Of course, they also found time for lovemaking, which was easier now that the twins were sleeping through the night. It was also a good time for them to talk about the day and share any news or information they had for one another.

"Well, what do you think, John?"

John sat up against his pillow, looking at his wife in his "Thinker" mode. "For one thing, I think that horse lady Donald nicknamed that patron had a lot of nerve, but you won't be seeing her again. Not only did Sheila ban her, but the woman made a spectacle of herself."

"I don't think she cared, John, but I'm more concerned about what happened in Sheila's office while she was gone. What do you think the professor was up to?"

John smiled. "Alicia, don't let your imagination run away with you. From what you said, the man wasn't perplexed at all when you confronted him. I'm sure his explanation was right. What other reason would he have to search Sheila's desk?"

Alicia sighed. This wasn't the first time John ignored her intuition, and in all those other cases, it had turned out to be right. "I don't know, John. He's too smooth an operator in my opinion. We don't know anything about him other than he knows Sheila's daughter."

"Then why don't you talk with her? Give her a call if that'll ease your mind."

"I don't think that's appropriate, John."

"Then use your research skills to check him out."

Alicia pondered that suggestion. "I've already googled him, and everything seems on the up and up. He does work at UCLA in the English Department."

"See? He's not a killer."

She tapped his arm. "I'm sure there are plenty of professors who have turned out to be killers."

"Maybe in mystery novels. Talking of which, why don't we get started on Chapter 4? Mary Lou wants to see a first draft next month." He took his laptop off the table next to the bed and opened it.

"I'm beginning to think Mary Lou is just as demanding as her sister was." Alicia wasn't convinced Professor Ryan Anderson was as innocent as John thought. Picking up her laptop, she joined John in working on Book 3 of their series, but she made a note to herself that she would continue to investigate Sheila's new boyfriend. Maybe when Gilly returned the next day she could recruit her into helping, as well. Gilly had proven her talent for detection last fall, but it had almost cost her and Alicia their lives. Since then, Gilly had promised Ramsay, with pinkies crossed behind her back, that she wouldn't interfere with any of his cases. Now that she was a married woman, Alicia wondered if her best friend would be different. She sincerely hoped not. A ring on her finger and a week in Hawaii couldn't change Abigail Nostran—Abigail Ramsay now—any more than a leopard could change its spots.

Chapter Four

Alicia awoke to the shrilling of the phone. Groggily, she reached out to get it afraid it might wake the twins. John didn't stir. She always joked he could sleep through a hurricane. Picking it up, she glanced at the illuminated light of her alarm clock. It read 4 a.m. Who would be calling at this hour? A tingle of fear raced up her spine. Had Mac or Betty taken ill? Her father-in-law and his girlfriend were both in their eighties. Although fit and spry despite the fact they both walked with canes and Mac's memory was on a decline, she worried about them.

"Hello," she whispered hoping it was a wrong number or a crank call. Her heart beat rapidly, waiting for the person on the other end to reply.

"Morning, Alicia." Oh, God. It was Gilly. Her breathing slowed, but now she was confused. "Gilly. Where are you? Isn't it earlier in Hawaii?"

"I'm not in Hawaii. I'm home at the inn. I couldn't sleep. I hope I didn't wake you."

Alicia contained a laugh. "You did, but it's okay. How was the honeymoon?"

"It was incredible. You and John should really go to the islands. Ron and I would be happy to watch Carol and Johnny, and you know the boys love the twins." She was babbling almost as much as Alicia's daughter.

"Well, I'm glad you're back. Is Ron there with you at the inn now?" Besides Edith and Rose, Alicia was the only one Gilly had told about the elopement. She'd sworn her to secrecy until they were out of town and given her their hotel number in Maui in case of any emergencies.

"Of course. I told you he agreed to move in here with us and give up that small apartment he rented when he moved to Cobble Cove. He was worried the guests might not like the idea of a sheriff on the premises, but it's as good as a watch dog." She giggled.

"Talking about a watch dog, I bet Ruby's happy you're back."

"Sure is. Edith and Rose spoiled her as badly as me and the boys do. By the way, Alicia, I brought back gifts for everyone including Sneaky."

"Sneaky? What did you get him, catnip?"

"Nope. Something better." Gilly paused. "I'd like to invite you to the inn for breakfast this morning. Can you bring him along, so I can give it to him personally?"

Alicia found this a strange request. There were times Sneaky stayed over her house or Laura's when the library was closed but other than the time he disappeared in the fall, the cat didn't make visits outside the library.

"I don't know, Gilly. The library doesn't open until nine today, and I'm working. I know you're not back yet, but I could drop over on my way and pick up Sneaky's gift and bring it to him."

"No. That would ruin the surprise. Doesn't Gladys open the library at eight? Couldn't you get in then, bring Sneaky to the inn, and take him back after you've had breakfast with us?"

Alicia should've known Gilly would be persistent. She wasn't one who gave up easily when she had a plan.

"Okay, Gilly. I think this is ridiculous, and Sheila might be upset if she finds out I came in early and took Sneaky, but I'd love to see you. Is John invited, too?"

"Yes, and Carol and Johnny, of course. If it's easier, ask John to take the twins while you pick up Sneaky."

"Does Ramsay know about this?" Alicia still called the sheriff by his last name.

"Not yet. He's sleeping, but don't worry. I learned quite a few more tricks on our honeymoon to persuade him to go along with my whims. I'll teach them to you if you want."

Alicia laughed. "I think I'm doing okay with John but thanks. What time should we be there?"

"John can come at eight, and you can meet him here as soon as you have Sneaky. I know you'll be in a rush, but I doubt Sheila will mind if you're a few minutes late. The last time we spoke, you mentioned she has a boyfriend. I can't wait to hear all about that and all the other library gossip."

Now it was clear why Gilly had asked Alicia over the day after she returned from her trip. She wanted to be prepared for when she went back to work the next day. When Gilly had called Alicia to let her know they'd gotten into Hawaii safe and given her their room number at the Maui Hilton, Alicia had mentioned the professor from California who'd appeared on the scene to work with Sheila on his book research. The way Gilly's mind worked, she predicted that he would become her boyfriend, and Alicia had to admit it looked like she was right.

*** *

When John got up at six, Alicia was already dressed.

"You're up early," he said slipping out of bed. "Should I wake the twins and start breakfast?"

That was their usual routine, but Gilly's invitation would disrupt their schedule this morning.

"No. Gilly and Ramsay are back at the inn. She called early and invited us to breakfast. She wants me to pick up Sneaky at the library first and said you could bring the twins before that at eight."

John's brows knit together. "Sneaky? What is she up to? Can you get into the library that early?"

"The custodian opens at eight, but I'm not thrilled about doing this without Sheila's permission. I'll bring the carrier we use when we take Sneaky home and a can of extra cat food we keep here to entice him to come with me, but I'm as curious as you to know why Gilly wants Sneaky brought to the inn. She said something about a present she wanted to give him. She also has gifts for all of us."

"A catnip mouse would be easy enough to bring him at the library."

"That's what I told her, but she says that's not what she got him."

"Hmmm. Well, I never refuse a free meal. She's almost as good a cook as you are."

Alicia laughed. "You know that Edith and Rose are the ones who make most of the breakfasts, John, and Ramsay sometimes picks up donuts even though he's trying to maintain his weight loss. I wonder how he did in Hawaii?"

"I'm sure they were getting plenty of exercise if you know what I mean." John grinned, displaying his dimple.

Alicia tapped him on his pajama sleeve. "Get dressed. I'll take care of the twins. Maybe I'll give them some cereal to tide them over until they get to the inn. They're used to eating at seven."

***

After John took off to the inn with Johnny and Carol buckled in their car seats in the back of his pickup, Alicia drove her own car to the library. She couldn't understand why Gilly had sent her on such a strange errand and was worried that Sheila wouldn't be pleased about it if she found out. The director was often at work before the library opened. Luckily, her car wasn't in the parking lot when Alicia arrived.

Toting her cat carrier, Alicia approached the library's automatic doors. She, like the other librarians, had a key, but she saw Gladys through the glass and waved at her. The custodian stopped polishing the front desk and walked to Alicia. Opening the door with a key on her keyring, rag still in hand, Gladys asked, "Hey, you're here early. What's up, Alicia, and why the cat carrier? I just fed Sneaky. He doesn't have a vet visit today, does he?"

"No. I just need to bring him to the inn for a short time, Gladys. Please don't say anything to Sheila. I'll have him back before the library opens."

"The inn? Do Edith and Rose want him for something? No, wait, is Gilly back?"

Alicia stepped into the library. "Yes, she is. She called me early this morning and invited me to breakfast, but she asked me to bring Sneaky. I don't know why."

Gladys smiled. "I like that lady even though she can be a bit crazy at times. No offense. She livens up this place when she's around."

"That she does," Alicia agreed. "Let me get Sneaky, so I can get over there and back in time to start work. Remember, not a word to Sheila."

"Mum's the word. I swear." She crossed her heart as Alicia hurried past.

***

Sneaky was asleep upstairs in his cat room, having already eaten the food that Gladys had put out for him. That made it easier for Alicia to pick him up, push him into the carrier, latch the door shut, and carry him to her car. Gladys gave her the thumbs-up sign, finger to her lips, as she relocked the library door behind her.

Sneaky didn't start crying until they were halfway to the inn. "Shhh, boy," Alicia said. "Gilly has a surprise for you. I have no idea what it is, but it better be something worth taking you from the library this morning."

When they arrived at the inn, Sneaky's plaintive meows had mellowed down to short cries. Alicia hefted his carrier up the porch steps. She was about to knock on the door when Gilly opened it and came out to greet her. Her friend from Long Island who had relocated to Cobble Cove last year was dressed unseasonably in a sleeveless multicolored flowered Hawaiian dress, a red lei around her neck. She had a golden tan that radiated from her normally pale skin.

"Good morning, Alicia," she chirped. "You just missed Ron. He took the boys to school and then insisted on getting back to work. He kept checking in with his officers while we were away, but I had my means of getting his attention back to his new wife." She grinned. "Come on in and bring Sneaky. I can't wait to see what he thinks of his surprise."

As Alicia entered, she saw John and the twins seated in the breakfast nook. The three of them each had a lei of a different color around their necks. "Mommy's here," John told Carol and Johnny, "and she's brought Sneaky."

"Sneaky," Carol yelled. Johnny put out his hand and petted the air. Now that the cat was safely inside, he had stopped crying completely. Alicia was hesitant to open his carrier. She placed it down by the entrance to the room.

"You can release him," Gilly said. "All the doors are closed."

"Not yet. Let me have a quick bite to eat and when you're ready to bring out his surprise, I'll let him out of the carrier."

"I think that's a good idea."

She sat next to John where a place was set with a glass of orange juice and a plate of muffins and Gilly's famous chocolate chip cookies. A yellow lei was draped on the back of the chair, obviously meant for her, so she put it on.

"Would you like some tea or coffee?" Gilly offered. "I know you have to get back to the library soon, but it's really good to see you. I can't wait to hear about everything that happened while I was away."

"You haven't missed much, Gilly. How was the honeymoon? You look wonderful."

Gilly blushed under her tan. "I feel great. We had a wonderful time in Maui. You two really must go one day." She glanced at John. "I have more souvenirs for you both and a few things for the kids, too. You can open them at home later, but I really would like to bring out Sneaky's surprise now." Before Alicia could comment, Gilly rushed away from the table.

"Did you want coffee, Ali?" John asked.

"No, the orange juice is fine. I'll have coffee at work later." She bit into a cookie. "Where's Edith and Rose?"

"Gilly said she told them to go home. Rose was staying here while she and Ramsay were on their honeymoon. There weren't many guests at this time of year after the Christmas fair people went home."

Alicia recalled how pleasant their annual event had gone this year compared to lasts. John had again acted as Santa Claus for the town's and visiting children. Carol and Johnny had now recognized it was their father, but they still believed the "real" Santa would deliver gifts to them on Christmas Eve.

"Take Sneaky out of his carrier, please," Gilly called from down the hall.

"I'll do it," John said rising from his chair. "You finish eating, Ali. This sounds like it's going to be some surprise." He winked.

"Suhpize," Carol cried. Johnny nearly toppled his travel highchair as he edged closer to the cat carrier anticipating Sneaky's escape.

With a deft motion, John clicked open the tabs on the top and bottom of the carrier. As he did at the vets, Sneaky refused to move but edged himself further back in the box.

"Sneaky's free, Gilly, but he's not coming out," John called.

"Let's see if he does now," Gilly said, entering the room. In her arms, bundled in the folds of her Hawaiian dress, was a tiny calico kitten.

"Oh, my gosh, Gilly!" Alicia said, almost choking on her cookie. "I don't believe it. You brought a cat back from Hawaii. How did you manage that?" She was thinking about the quarantines and airline procedures.

"I have my ways," she said rolling her eyes provocatively. "The check-in clerks and the captain found me quite alluring. Ron was jealous, but I got us a kitty. I found her on the beach, poor thing. I think she'll make a great inn cat." She brought the kitten over to the table. The twins went wild. "Kitty, Kitty," they both called, reaching out. She handed the cat to Alicia who let Carol and Johnny pet her.

"It's a little girl," Alicia said, examining the backside of the kitten.

"Yep. Her name is KittyKai. 'Kai' means 'sea' in Hawaiian."

"Pretty, the name and the cat. I never had a calico."

"You should get a cat. The twins will be old enough soon to have a pet."

"I think Sneaky's enough for us," John said, "and Fido when Dad brings him by."

"Speaking of Sneaky," Gilly said, "Look!" She pointed at the carrier where a beige head was peeking out. Slowly, the Siamese ambled out.

Gilly picked up KittyKai and placed her on the ground.

"Gilly, I don't think..." Alicia was alarmed that Sneaky might harm the kitten. Instead, he sniffed her. KittyKai, however, drew her small body back, black, orange, and white fur standing on end, her tail erect—the signs of confrontation. She hissed in Sneaky's face.

Gilly went to grab her, but Alicia stopped her. "No. Leave them alone. You don't get in the middle of a cat fight."

"They're not fighting, Alicia. They're getting to know one another."

Sneaky backed away into his carrier. He was obviously not charmed by his "gift." KittyKai, having won the small battle, skittered to Gilly.

"It's going to take some time. You should bring Sneaky over more often. I was hoping they could be friends."

"Gilly, Sneaky's neutered."

"Not those type of friends, Alicia. Is that all you think is on my mind?"

Alicia chose not to answer that question. "What does Ruby think of the new kitten?" Ruby was Gilly's old beagle.

As if in answer to Alicia's question, the dog strolled into the room and lay down. KittyKai joined her, and the two snuggled together by the back door.

"How cute. I wonder how Fido will react to KittyKai."

"I'm going to invite Mac over later and see."

"Well, that was an interesting surprise," Alicia said, glancing up at the kitchen clock, "but I have to get back to the library with Sneaky." She got up, gave John a quick kiss on the lips and the twins each a kiss on their foreheads. Carol and Johnny were still munching on cookies, and John said he'd bring them home as soon as they were done.

"Let me give you a hand with Sneaky's carrier, and I can walk you out," Gilly offered. She bent down and latched the cat carrier. Sneaky peered at her through the slats. "Silly boy, afraid of my little kitty. I'm sure you'll love her once you get to know her."

Alicia laughed. "I knew it. You're matchmaking them."

Gilly smiled as she picked up the carrier. "I admit it. I'm a romantic at heart."

"Speaking of being romantic," Alicia said, "I didn't get a chance to tell you that Sheila and Nancy are planning Valentine's Day Parties at the library on Friday. There'll be one for the patrons and another for the staff and their families after work."

"Sounds like fun. I hope Ron can join us. We have some special plans of our own that night, but if things are slow at the station, maybe he can pick me up and we can spend a few minutes at the party."

Gilly, still toting the cat carrier with Sneaky inside, allowed Alicia to hold the door open for her, and they stepped out on to the inn's porch. An elderly woman bundled up in a heavy coat sat there knitting in a rocker.

"Mrs. Burke," Gilly greeted her. "It's cold out here. Why don't you go inside and have some muffins and cookies? If you want, I can fry up some eggs with toast for you, too."

The gray-haired woman looked up from her needlework. "I'm fine, Mrs. Ramsay. The sun's out, and it's warm for February. I'm not much of a breakfast eater, and I helped myself to some fruit this morning. I didn't want to disturb you when you were entertaining your friends."

Gilly shook her head. "I consider all my guests friends. By the way, this is Alicia McKinney. She works with me at the library."

The woman stood up, placing her handiwork, several rows of knitted blue yarn, on the table next to her chair. "Nice to meet you, Mrs. McKinney. I'm Cecelia Burke. I just checked into this delightful inn a few days ago. I'm a retired widow. I lost my husband in October. He never liked to do much traveling, so I decided now was the time for me to see the country. I'm particularly interested in small towns like Cobble Cove. I never liked the hectic pace of cities."

"Sorry to hear about your husband," Alicia said. "Where are you originally from, Mrs. Burke?"

"Please call me Cecelia. I've lived in several places. My husband, despite the fact he hated travel, was in the service. We moved around quite a bit. After he retired, we settled in New Jersey."

Alicia glanced at her watch, again remembering the time. "Sorry to cut our talk short, Cecelia, but I have to get to work. Will you be staying in town much longer?"

"Not sure right now, Alicia. I can call you that, right?"

"Of course."

"I should be here at least until next week."

"Great. Then maybe we'll be able to chat again. If you'd like, please stop by the library. We don't have a lot of attractions to offer in Cobble Cove, but if you enjoy reading, we have a very good library if I say so myself." She smiled. "And a nice collection of craft books, including many on knitting."

Cecelia laughed. "I may take you up on that, Alicia. Now don't let me make you late for your job." She glanced at the carrier Alicia had taken from Gilly. "Is that a kitty in there you're bringing with you? Pretty, a Siamese. I bet she's your library cat."

"She's a he," Alicia corrected. "and, yes, he's the Cobble Cove library cat."

Sneaky suddenly let out a terrible hiss from his carrier.

"What's going on with Sneaky?" Alicia asked. "He was so quiet up until now. KittyKai is still in the house with Ruby, isn't she?"

Gilly nodded. "Yes. It's strange." Sneaky began to buck the carrier as if he wanted to escape. Alicia put it down. "Maybe he needs to rest a minute."

"Let me help you with him," Cecelia offered. But before she could pick up the box, Sneaky let out an even louder yowl.

"What's wrong, boy?" Alicia asked, bending down to face the wild-eyed cat. She noticed he was staring in the direction of Cecelia Burke.

Chapter Five

"Awww. It's okay, kitty. No one is going to hurt you," Cecelia said, stepping away from the carrier. "I had cats when my son was at home, and they always associated going to the vet with being placed in their cat carriers. I'm sure he'll settle down once he's back in the library."

Alicia picked up the carrier. "Yes, he normally cries when we bring him to Dr. Clark, but nothing like this. It's as if something spooked him."

As Alicia turned the carrier away from Cecelia, Sneaky quieted down. "Maybe you're right, and he just wants to get back to his comfy spot at the library." She secretly wished she'd asked Laura, the consummate cat handler and children's librarian, to help her bring Sneaky to the inn, but his behavior had been fine up until their departure.

Gilly walked Alicia to her car and helped her put the carrier in the back seat. Sneaky remained quiet as she got behind the wheel and waved goodbye to Gilly and Cecelia. She was cutting it close to the library's opening time, so she didn't have much of an opportunity to ponder Sneaky's reaction. She sped down Bookshelf Lane hoping none of Ramsay's men were patrolling the area. All she needed was a ticket to hold her up further.

Luckily, Sheila's car wasn't parked in the lot when Alicia pulled in. Gerry raised an eyebrow as she entered carrying Sneaky. "Hi, Alicia. Gladys warned me you'd taken the cat. Good thing Sheila's not early this morning. After what happened in the fall, she hates people getting here before me and Gladys."

"I know, and I tried to be quick. I was held up a few minutes at the inn."

"Is that where you were? Is Gilly back?"

"Yes. John, the twins, and I had breakfast with her. I also met one of her guests. She might stop by here later."

Gerry ran a hand through his sandy crew cut. "I thought all the guests were gone. The inn empties out around this time."

"Well, this lady is a retired widow. She says she enjoys visiting small towns. She was out on the porch knitting and didn't seem to mind the cold. I suggested she come check out some of our craft books."

"Hmm." Gerry narrowed his blue eyes. "Sounds like a Madame Defarge to me."

Alicia laughed. Since Gerry started as security guard at the library after the events last winter, he'd taken up reading library classics. She knew his current book was *A Tale of Two Cities*.

"I doubt that, Gerry, but Sneaky didn't take too well to her for some reason."

"See. She may be as loony as that horse woman."

They'd walked toward the elevator. "Has Mrs. Kleisman been back?" She wondered if the irate patron who'd thrown coffee at Sheila had returned to the library at night after her shift.

Gerry shook his head. "No, but I've been warned to keep an eye out for her. She's not allowed to enter this building."

As Alicia pressed the up button to bring Sneaky back upstairs, Gerry added, "There's a bunch of donuts in the break room if you're still hungry. I brought them in for coffee break."

Alicia smiled and gave him a thumbs up with her free hand. The elevator doors opened, and she pulled Sneaky's carrier inside. The Siamese remained silent.

Satisfied with herself for getting Sneaky back in the nick of time, Alicia released him into his cat room where he promptly took up his place again on his cat tree. She then grabbed her favorite donut, a Boston Cream, and a napkin from the break room, and headed down to the Reference Desk. Donald was already there browsing Facebook. "Hey, Alicia, no eating at the desk," he warned teasingly.

"Hey, Donald, no personal Internet surfing at the desk," she countered.

He laughed. "Is Gilly back yet? I need someone with better verbal fencing skills."

Alicia joined him behind the desk, tossing the remainder of her donut, the part without the chocolate and cream, into the nearby trash can. "I thought that was rather good. And, yes, Gilly came home last night. I saw her briefly this morning. She'll be in tomorrow."

"I hope she brought me a nice Hawaiian tie," he said, adjusting his plain red one.

"I have no idea, but she gave me, John, and the twins leis. I left mine in the car. I didn't want it to clash with your tie."

He grinned. "That's better." Before they could continue their verbal sparring, Sheila walked through the door with Nancy. The two were chatting about the Valentine's party.

"I've placed an order for heroes with Duncan, and Claire's making the cake."

"Perfect," Sheila said. "and be sure to send a press release to the papers in the surrounding area and give Alicia one to bring home to John for the *Courier*."

"Sounds like your plans are shaping up," Alicia said as Nancy and Sheila came to the desk. It was still a few minutes before Gladys would open the door to patrons.

Sheila's eyes were bright, nearly matching her emerald blouse. "Yes. Nancy is doing a wonderful job. When Abigail returns, maybe I can also persuade her to bring some of her chocolate chip cookies to the party. That might be a way of diverting attention from our real purpose of celebrating her marriage."

"Nice idea. You can run it by her tomorrow. I saw her earlier, and she looks great."

"You didn't give it away, did you, Alicia?"

"Oh, no. I'm much better at keeping secrets than Gilly. Don't worry, Sheila. The only one you might need to be concerned with is Donald."

"Stop that, Alicia." Donald tapped his mouse on its pad. "I've had enough teasing for today. I'm very good at keeping secrets."

Sheila was about to comment, when two raised voices came from outside.

"You were told not to step foot in this establishment. That includes hanging around outside the library." It was Gerry.

"I can hang out wherever I like. I'm a Cobble Cove resident, and I pay your taxes, young man." The second voice was clearly Mrs. Kleisman's.

"Oh, no. She's back," Nancy said. "I heard what happened yesterday, Sheila. What's wrong with that woman?"

"The horse isn't giving up," Donald said.

Sheila turned around. "Let's see about that."

"No, Sheila. Let Gerry take care of this, or we can call Ramsay. He's back at the station today." Alicia was afraid of another confrontation between the two women.

Sheila stopped in her tracks. "You're right, Alicia, but calling the sheriff isn't the answer. She's just asking for attention. We need to ignore her."

Through the library windows, the staff and patrons entering the library watched as Ryan Anderson appeared on the scene.

"Mr. Fox, are you having a problem with this woman?"

"Professor Anderson. I've warned Mrs. Kleisman to leave this area, and she isn't complying with my request."

"Is that so?" Even though the security guard had a few inches over Anderson, the professor pushed out his chest and glared down at Mrs. Kleisman. "You listen to Mr. Fox, ma'am, and vacate these premises."

"Ah ha. You think you can use your fancy words on me, Professor. I know you're just showing off to your girlfriend."

Sheila rushed outside as she saw Anderson launch himself at Rhonda Kleisman, shoving her aside, away from the door. "You're lucky I didn't punch you for that remark. Now get out of here."

"I sure will, Mr. Professor, and you can expect to hear from my lawyer later today." She looked at Sheila, who'd put an arm out to restrain Ryan. "As for you, Director Whitehead, you haven't heard the last from me either. I don't get mad, I get even." She walked off.

"That lady's trouble," Donald said to Alicia.

"Yes, but the Professor had no right to push her," Nancy said. "It's a side of him I don't think Sheila has ever seen."

The staff members stopped talking as Ryan and Sheila walked back in the building. "I'm so sorry," Ryan said to Sheila. "I don't know what possessed me. I'm a man of words, not violence. I've never touched a woman before in anger."

Sheila faced him. "It's alright, Ryan. Don't blame yourself. She provoked you."

From experience with the few irate patrons the library had dealt with since she began working there, Alicia knew Sheila would be filing an incident report about Mrs. Kleisman with the Board. Whether the woman would go through with her threat to have her lawyer stage a complaint against the professor or if she was serious about taking revenge on Sheila was yet to be seen.

Chapter Six

Sheila called an emergency board meeting. Mac, Betty, Edith, and Rose met behind closed doors with her, Gerry, and Ryan in the meeting room.

"I wish I could be a fly on that wall," Donald commented after the group arrived and headed upstairs.

Alicia felt no desire to eavesdrop. She knew what they were discussing and that Sheila would keep them all in the loop once she had the decision of the Board.

An hour later, Nancy came to the desk. She was holding a sheaf of paper. "Sheila asked me to distribute this memo to the staff.

"Let's see. Let's see," Donald said, holding out his hand like an eager boy waiting to open his birthday or Christmas present.

"Calm down, Donald. This isn't a winning lottery ticket." Nancy gave him the paper and then handed one to Alicia before heading to the Children's room.

"Listen to this," Donald said, reading aloud even though Alicia had her own copy:

In response to the incident on the morning of February 12, the library staff is instructed to call the sheriff's office (the number is listed next to the reference desk) if Mrs. Rhonda Kleisman enters the library or the library property including the outside areas. These instructions must be followed without any word or action on the part of a library employee toward Mrs. Kleisman or any patron who has become involved. If anyone has any questions about this procedure, please contact the director.

"And it's signed by Sheila and the members of the Board."

"Thanks, Donald, but I can read. I think it's appropriate to the situation. I only wonder if Mrs. Kleisman plans to sue Ryan and/or the library."

"I wouldn't put anything past that woman."

"Hello, there."

Alicia turned to see Betty and Mac walking toward the reference desk, tipping their canes in rhythm. It always delighted her to see the old couple.

"Sorry we didn't stop to say hello earlier," Betty said. "Sheila was in such a tizzy we didn't want to disrupt her. She's in her office now with Ryan. I think she's upset with him, but I don't blame him for how he reacted toward that horrible woman."

"Allowing one's temper to explode is never the answer, Betty. Two wrongs don't make things right."

Mac had a habit of rephrasing euphemisms to his own liking.

"That's a stupid saying, Jonathan. I think people need to express themselves."

Before her father-in-law and his girlfriend started a fight, Alicia asked, "Where's Fido?"

"I left him at home. Sheila wouldn't appreciate my bringing him to a board meeting, but Laura has him scheduled for another children's story time with Sneaky next week."

"Oh, good. The kids really love him."

Mac turned to Betty. "What do you say we get going home now, honeybuns? It's not yet Valentine's, but any day is a good one for romance." He winked at Alicia. "I hope John picked up that lesson from his dad."

Alicia felt herself beginning to blush. "The answer is 'yes,' Mac, and I thank you for teaching him well."

"My pleasure. Have a good day, Alicia."

A few minutes after the couple ambled away, Edith and Rose appeared at the desk.

"Hello, Alicia, Donald," Edith said. Rose, in her usual quiet manner, simply nodded at them.

"Nice to see you," Alicia said. Donald had his nose in Facebook.

"I hear you were by the inn with Gilly this morning," Edith continued. "Don't you adore her new kitty?"

"Kitty?" Donald looked up from his screen. "You didn't tell me Gilly got a cat. You know how I feel about felines. I come this close to dropping a paper bag over Sneaky and dumping him in the cove."

Alicia rolled her eyes. "Stop the pretense, Donald, I know you like Sneaky. Gilly brought KittyKai back from Hawaii. She's a pretty calico kitten."

"What kind of name is that?" Donald said. "If I had a cat, I'd name him Tom or Jerry or maybe Garfield."

"So original. I think it's a wonderful name. 'Kai' means ocean in Hawaiian and they named her that because they found her on a beach."

Edith added, "I think it's great to have a cat at the inn. Not that we get many mice or bugs, but they add a nice homey touch to the place, and they're great for kids."

"I never had a pet," Donald said. "and I turned out fine."

Alicia tried to hide her laugh. "Did Sheila or Nancy mention Friday's party to you two ladies?" she asked changing the subject.

"Nancy did, and we're looking forward to it, although we don't celebrate Valentine's Day. We're a bit past that stage in our lives. Aren't we, Rose?" Rose nodded, and Edith continued. "Not that we wouldn't consider a fling if the right man turned up. I mean, look at Betty and Sheila. They're no spring chickens. Right, Rose?"

This time, the younger sister replied in a whisper. "No, Edie. They're not."

"Well, while we're here we might as well check out some books." Edith turned and headed toward the craft section while Rose waved weakly back at them and followed her.

There was someone else browsing the craft books. Alicia recognized the curly gray head and layered blue coat of Cecelia Burke, Gilly's inn guest, as she thumbed through the knitting books.

"Excuse me, Donald," she said as she left the desk and walked to the 735 section.

"Hello, Mrs. Burke. I see you took me up on visiting here as you promised earlier."

The woman placed the "Perl One Step by Step" book back on the shelf and turned to Alicia. "Yes. I didn't realize how close the inn is to the library. It was a pleasant walk despite a slight chill."

"Can I help you find anything?" Alicia noticed Edith had already chosen a few books and had brought Rose over to the baking aisle. She imagined that even if Claire was supplying the party cake, Rose might whip up a wonderful dessert, too.

"No. I'm just looking. Thank you. Is your director around?"

"She's in her office right now. She just came out of a meeting. Is there a reason you want to see her?"

"No. I'm just curious as to who runs this beautiful library. As I told you, I'm enchanted with small towns. That includes their libraries, schools, and shops."

"You'll love Cobble Corner then," Alicia said. "Have you been there yet?"

"No, but it's on my agenda. Gilly says she shops there often. She advised me to try Chloe's Closet. She says they have lovely styles at a decent price."

"Gilly is quite a shopper," Alicia agreed. "I'll be back at the desk if you need anything. Since you're not a resident, you won't be able to check out any books, but I could put them on Gilly's card if you want. I'd have to call and get her permission."

"No. That won't be necessary. I'm only looking at patterns. If I like one, I can always photocopy it." She glanced at the copiers by the front doors.

Alicia went back to Donald who was messaging Roger on Facebook.

"Donald, get back to work," she said in mock imitation of Sheila.

"Who was that?" he asked. "Was it Madame Defarge?"

She laughed. "That's what Gerry calls her. Her name is Cecelia Burke, and she's very nice."

"Do you want to know your nickname, Alicia?"

"Definitely not, Tie Man."

Donald chuckled as he logged out of Facebook and opened the online catalog. For once, he was listening to her.

***

The rest of the day went uneventfully. When Alicia arrived home, John was setting the table for dinner. The twins were propped up in their high chairs playing with their kid-sized utensils. She smelled something delicious simmering on the stove. The scent of garlic and onions permeated the air.

"John, that smells delicious."

He turned and smiled, came over and gave her a kiss. "Thank you. It's Mom's pasta sauce. I'm cooking us spaghetti and meatballs tonight. I'm using some of Dad's herbs. I also made one of Mac's special appetizers – fresh bruschetta."

"Sounds yummy." Alicia returned his kiss and then gave kisses to the twins. John stirred the sauce pot and then brought the warm bruschetta to the table.

"I'll have to cut this up for the twins. I hope they can handle this bread. It's a bit hard to chew."

"I think they should be able to. They've already gotten a bunch of baby teeth." Alicia took a bite of the bread to test it. "Not that hard, and it sure is tasty. These herbs and the tomatoes are so fresh. How did you manage that in the middle of winter?"

"You know how good Dad is at canning, Ali. He gave me a stock recently. It's hard to believe it's not just out of the garden."

When the food was ready, and they sat down to eat, John asked Alicia how her day went after she left the inn.

"It was crazy, John. That woman, Mrs. Kleisman, that I told you about who threw coffee on Sheila, she was hanging around outside the library. Gerry ordered her off the property, but she wouldn't listen. Professor Anderson showed up and had a few words with her. She said something about Ryan showing off in front of his girlfriend, and he exploded. He pushed her away. Luckily, she wasn't hurt. She threatened to sue, though, and said she'd get even with Sheila, too."

"That doesn't sound good." John paused in twirling spaghetti around Johnny's fork. "I don't know Professor Anderson well, but he doesn't strike me as someone with a temper. I understand how that woman would've provoked him, but I can't condone striking a woman under any circumstances."

"I knew you'd feel that way, John. Sheila called a special meeting of the Board to discuss the situation. Nancy then distributed a memo instructing the staff to call the sheriff if Mrs. Kleisman comes on the property again."

John handed the wrapped fork to his son. "And what was done about Anderson?"

"Nothing." She reached into her purse that she'd hung behind her chair and took out a paper that she handed to him. "Read it. I brought it home, so you could see."

John scanned the memo. "Hmmm. That's strange. In my opinion, Kleisman just may have a case against Anderson and against the library, too."

Alicia recalled John had taken some courses in law before studying journalism.

"She wasn't injured, John, and she'd been banned from the library. If anything, Sheila could've sued her for nearly ruining her suit with that coffee."

"That's true, but I think Sheila is protecting Anderson because of her feelings for him. What do you know about this guy, anyway?"

"Now you sound like Donald. He asked me the same thing. You men are so suspicious. We already verified he's a legit professor from California, and he knows Sheila's daughter."

"Why don't you call her and confirm that?"

"John, stop. I've never spoken to the woman. You're being ridiculous."

At Alicia's tone, John knew to change the subject. "What else happened today?"

"Not much after that. Oh, but this morning . . ." Alicia straightened the bib on Carol who was spattering sauce off her spoon.

"When Gilly walked me out of the inn, I met one of her guests. She was sitting outside knitting. Her name is Cecilia Burke. She recently lost her husband and is traveling around small towns. She says she likes them better than cities. She came to the library today to check out some craft books, but she just made copies of patterns. She wasn't there too long."

John made the blank face that indicated he was bored.

"The odd thing, John, is that while Gilly was helping me bring Sneaky out, he went berserk when he saw Mrs. Burke. He hardly ever reacts to people that way."

"Well, he didn't take well to KittyKai. Maye he was keyed up from that."

"KittyKai was the one who hissed and fattened her tail at him."

John laughed. "Now you're the one acting suspicious, Ali. I caught a glimpse of that woman you mentioned as I was bringing the twins home. She looked like a sweet old lady."

"Donald called her Madame Defarge, and he hasn't even met her."

John wiped Johnny's mouth and placed a sliced meatball on his highchair tray. "Let's just enjoy our dinner and stop gossiping about people. You didn't ask about my day, but it was productive. While the twins were watching cartoons, I managed to crank out another chapter in our book. It's your turn next, so you might want to read it later."

Alicia and John alternated chapters when they cowrote their Groucho Marx mystery series, but if one of them got blocked, the other was always ready to pick up the slack.

"I'll be sure to do that, John. On a happier note, the plans for the Valentine's Day parties at the library are coming along well. Nancy made the prettiest fliers and pasted them all over the place. Gilly and Ramsay will be surprised when they learn the staff event is in their honor."

John grinned. "Knowing Gilly, she'll ferret that information out of you tomorrow when she comes back to work. Your friend has a knack for making people reveal their secrets."

"That's true, John. Maybe that's why she and Ramsay hooked up. His job is to solve crimes, and she's a regular Miss Marple."

"Let's just hope that no crimes take place at the party."

Alicia thought of Mrs. Kleisman's words to Sheila and cringed. So far, the woman hadn't made her threatened moves against the professor or the director. But a happy occasion like the Valentine's Day party might be the perfect opportunity for her to seek her revenge.

Chapter Seven

Alicia managed to put her worry aside the next day when Gilly returned to work. Her friend breezed in, her tanned face glowing. She wore a red, heart-covered long-sleeved sweatshirt in honor of Valentine's Day and a pair of gray pants. Around her neck, she sported a white lei.

"I'm back," she announced as she strode over to the reference desk.

"Welcome back, Gilly," Donald said. Alicia noted his tie matched the design of Gilly's top.

"Thanks, Donald. I should've brought you a lei, but I thought a Hawaiian tie would be more your style. It's in my car with gifts for the rest of the staff. I'll distribute them at break."

"Thank you. It's good to have you back. I heard you picked up a cat on the beach during your trip."

Gilly smiled. "Yes, indeed. KittyKai is the sweetest little girl. Ron's in love with her."

Donald rolled his eyes. "Better watch out. You've got competition and from a cat no less." He made a face that showed he wasn't thrilled with the feline species.

Gilly laughed. "Believe me, honey, KittyKai is no competition for me. Ron and I made quite the waves on the beach and continue to rock the boat now that we're home if you know what I mean."

"Same old raunchy Gilly," Alicia said. "But the analogies are a bit over the top."

Gilly winked. "I take that as a compliment. Now tell me what I've missed, peoples. I hear Sheila's got a beau." She walked behind the desk and lowered her voice to a whisper. It was a quiet morning, and Gladys had not yet opened the library doors to admit the public.

"What do you know about this Professor guy? I can't wait to see him."

"You'll see him soon enough," Donald told her. "He hangs around here like a lost puppy."

"Now you're the one with the analogies."

"Whatever. Oooh, is that him?"

A few patrons had lined up by the entrance. Alicia was happy to see Mrs. Kleisman wasn't among them. The first in line was Ryan Anderson toting books under his arm and a single rose in a tissue-paper wrapper in his other hand.

"Geez, he's bringing her a flower," Donald said under his breath.

"That's so sweet. He's a looker."

Alicia had to admit the Professor, although at least a half decade older than Ramsay, was in great shape and displayed quite a distinguished appearance.

Gladys arrived a few minutes later and unlocked the doors. The usual Thursday morning early risers filed in along with the professor. Adele Wexler made a beeline to the mystery section while the other patrons either asked Donald for a pass to use the computers or headed to different areas of the library. Ryan strode to the reference desk, smiling. "Good morning, Alicia, Donald." He paused when he noticed Gilly. "You must be the new Mrs. Ramsay. I've heard so much about you."

"I hope all good things. You must be Professor Anderson. I hear you're Sheila's boyfriend."

Alicia almost punched Gilly in the arm for her forthrightness, but Ryan didn't seem to mind. "Yes, I'm guilty of that. We started as colleagues on a project, but we've become a bit more involved than that. Is Sheila in her office?"

Alicia nodded, but as Ryan was about to step away toward the staircase, Donald, who had just handed the last patron the yellow slip with the log-on information for the library's PC's, said, "Excuse me, Professor, but I think you're a day early."

Ryan looked down at the flower he was holding. "Oh, you mean, this? No, it's not a Valentine's gift. I have something else planned for tomorrow. This is just a token of my appreciation for the way Sheila defended me against that horrid woman yesterday." "

Are you coming to the party?" Alicia asked. She assumed Sheila had invited him.

"Of course, but I may be running a little late. I have an appointment around that time. Sheila said I could attend the staff party. I should be able to make that."

"Great. John is also meeting me here after work. He's arranged for his father to watch the twins while we're at the library."

"Aren't Mac and Betty going anywhere for Valentine's?" Gilly asked.

"I think they're celebrating at home later."

"Got ya," Gilly said with a wink. After the Professor went upstairs to meet Sheila, Alicia asked Gilly what she thought of him.

"Smooth as silk, but I sense he's got some hidden rough spots. What happened between him and Mrs. Kleisman yesterday that Sheila had to defend him?"

Before Alicia could answer, Donald filled her in on the sordid incident in his own dramatic way. He ended with "and then Ryan punched horse lady in the face."

"Donald!" Alicia laughed. "All he did was push her."

"Still. You'd never think that guy had such a temper."

"Hmmm." Gilly pondered Donald's words. "Have you Googled him, Alicia?"

"Yes, and you're not the first person to ask me that. He checks out."

"Not everything can be found on the computer. Did you say he knows Sheila's daughter in California?"

"I did. That's how he found out about our library."

Gilly's "Hmmm" was louder this time. As a patron came to the desk with a question, Alicia couldn't help but wonder what that meant.

***

Right before morning break, Nancy approached the desk. As usual, she wore a handsomely tailored suit, this one a pretty shade of red closer to rose than scarlet. She had a white blouse underneath that was edged in delicate lace. A strand of pearls around her neck matched her earrings.

"Good morning, Alicia, Abigail, Donald," she greeted them.

"Hello, Nancy," Gilly said. She didn't allow too many people to address her by her actual first name, but she made an exception for the PR director. "I brought something back for you from Hawaii that will go perfect with that outfit. I'm distributing the staff gifts on break. Since everyone takes theirs at a different time, I'll leave the labelled bags upstairs after I get them from my car."

Nancy smiled. "Thank you. How nice of you to think of all of us. Did you have a nice honeymoon?"

Gilly raised her eyebrows. "What do you think, honey?"

Nancy nearly blushed under her ebony skin.

Alicia changed the subject. "So, Nance, do you have some jobs for us to prepare for the patron party tomorrow?" Alicia knew how organized Nancy was and how she was a master of delegation without being overbearing.

"In fact, I do, Alicia." She took a small pad out of her suit pants pocket. "Gilly, would you mind wrapping the Blind Date with a Book gifts? The books have already been chosen, and I have some beautiful Valentine's paper you can use. You can start after break. I'll bring everything out to you then."

"I'd love to help with that. As you know, I often volunteer with Edith and Rose to wrap gifts at the Christmas Fair. There's just one thing . . ."

Now Nancy was the one to quirk a dark, well tweezed eyebrow.

"If I find any bodice ripper books in the mix, I might take them myself."

"Oh, Gilly!" Alicia exclaimed. "You never get enough, do you?"

"Nope. Ron's a lucky man."

Ignoring that, Alicia asked, "How can I help?"

"You and Donald can hang some decorations. I'll ask Gladys to bring out the ladder. It would be nice to string the paper hearts across the reference and circulation desks and the entryway. Can you two handle that?"

Donald laughed. "It's a tough job, but someone's got to do it."

"How about the staff party?" Gilly asked. "Is that going to be upstairs?"

"Yes, but we don't have to set up for it until after the library closes. I have other people helping with that."

"Should I tell Ron to meet me here after five?"

Alicia saw Nancy hesitate with her reply. She hoped they could convince Gilly to go home and then come back or keep her downstairs until they'd finished the preparations for the surprise welcome home party for her and the sheriff.

Alicia needn't have worried. Nancy had already prepared for this question with the same idea Sheila had suggested earlier. "Gilly, we were hoping you could bring us some of those delicious cookies you bake for your sons' boy scout troop. The party won't start immediately after we close, so you have time to go back to the inn to pick them up. Don't rush back. We probably won't have things going until six."

"That sounds good. I'll be happy to bake the cookies, and it'll give me time to change and hook up with Ron at his office. You know how he runs late, anyway."

Alicia almost sighed with relief that Gilly had bought Nancy's excuse, or had she?" When Nancy walked away to recruit more helpers from the Children's Room, Gilly asked, "Is there something going on at the staff party that I don't know about?"

"Not that we know of, Gilly." Donald hid his face behind the computer.

"Hmmm," Gilly repeated. "I guess I'll take my break now and bring everyone's gifts in from my car."

"Do you need help?" Alicia asked.

"Yes, please. Otherwise, it will take a few trips."

"Should I ask Gladys for a hand truck?"

Gilly laughed. "No. They're not that big, and I have them in bags."

As Alicia headed out the library door with Gilly, she thought she saw someone by one of the bushes. But whoever had been there stepped away quickly out of sight around the building.

"That's strange," Alicia said as they walked to the parking lot.

"What?"

"Nothing. I thought I saw somebody by the bushes. When we walked by, they disappeared, but not into the library."

"I didn't see anything, Alicia. Maybe it was a kid. Is there a story time today?"

"No. They hold those on Tuesdays not Thursdays, and most of the kids are in school at this hour. I wonder if it was Mrs. Kleisman hanging around again. I really hope not."

"I wouldn't worry about her, Alicia. People like that are all bark and no bite."

"I hope you're right, Gilly, but something tells me we haven't heard the last of the horse lady."

Chapter Eight

When Gilly and Alicia were headed back into the library, they saw Ryan on his way out. "Have a nice day, ladies," he said. Alicia was surprised that his visit that morning had been so brief. After they smiled at the professor, Gilly whispered, "A quickie today, huh?"

Up in the break room, Gilly distributed the gifts she'd brought back for the staff from Hawaii: gardenia perfume for Sheila; a Hawaiian tie for Donald; a pretty floral notebook for Nancy; a hula skirt for Laura, a box of Macadamia nuts for Alicia, and assorted trinkets for the other library employees.

When they were downstairs, Alicia said, "You didn't have to get me the nuts, Gilly. John brought home the gifts you gave us yesterday. The Hawaiian fruit is delicious, and the kids loved the toys. Carol went crazy over the hula girl doll, and Johnny couldn't keep his hands off the toy ukulele."

"I forgot to give John the nuts. I don't think the kids can eat them, but you and John can share."

"Thanks. Just what I need when I was about to start my diet to get in shape for spring."

Gilly grinned. "No dieting until after Valentine's Day. Then I can join you. I gained a ton in Hawaii. That's why I've been wearing these caftans." She indicated the flowing blouse. Alicia knew her friend suffered from a lifelong battle with her weight, but she thought she looked slimmer since returning from her honeymoon. "You look great, Gilly. I'm sure you burned off all those extra calories by walking on the beach and other exercise." She winked.

Gilly smiled. "Well, you have a point there, but once the weather warms up, we should get together in the morning for some jogging around town."

"I don't know about jogging, but I've been taking Johnny and Carol for short walks before coming to work. Sometimes John comes with us after dinner. I suppose I could manage some time to exercise with you."

Nancy came up behind them, quiet in her flats. "Sorry to interrupt, but I'd love to join you two ladies. As you know, I often bicycle to work when there's no snow on the ground. I'm not far from the inn, and I could meet you both there in the morning a few times a week or whatever schedule is good for everyone."

Alicia eyed Nancy's neat, tailored suit and her long, lean body. She wondered how she managed not to wrinkle her clothes while bicycling, but she suspected the package she carried in her bicycle basket each day contained a steam iron as well as her lunch.

"That would be fun," Gilly said. "We could start a library exercise club. We could call it The Cobble Cove Cruisers or something like that."

Donald, listening in as he browsed his Facebook messages, said, "Roger is always after me to join his health club, but I know it would be a waste of money because I'd never stick to it. I wouldn't mind trying something like what you're talking about. Instead of driving to work, I could meet you guys at the inn and hoof it here."

Donald's choice of words brought Mrs. Kleisman to Alicia's mind. *Would they encounter the horse lady on their walks?*

"I suggest we start the Monday after Valentine's Day," Gilly said. "We could bundle up if it's too cold. Ron bought me the warmest fur coat before we went on our honeymoon. It's fake chinchilla. I haven't even had a chance to wear it yet."

Sheila came to the desk. "I know it's slow today, but you all seem to be doing more chatting than working. You also need to get tomorrow's party organized."

"Right," Gilly said. "I'll go wrap the Blind Date books now. Did you hear what we were discussing, Sheila? Maybe you'd like to exercise with us?"

Sheila, like Nancy, had a body that seemed immune to calories. "I'll think about it. Ryan's a runner, but my knees and back aren't up to that."

Alicia had forgotten that Sheila suffered from mild arthritis. "Walking might be okay," she said. "We'll all go at our own pace. It's supportive to exercise together."

Sheila nodded. "I guess so. Maybe I'll give it a try. Are you inviting the rest of the staff?"

"Yes," Gilly said. "I'll put a sign upstairs in the lounge. We'll meet at the inn and walk or jog to the library on workdays. Not everyone lives around here, but those who drive, like Laura, can park at the inn."

"Sounds good. Now get back to your jobs." Sheila walked away, tossing her red hair over her shoulders, the scent of her new perfume drifting back to them.

As Gilly left the desk to wrap the Blind Date books and no doubt look for some bodice rippers for herself, Alicia went to find Gladys for the ladder and party decorations. She'd forgotten to ask Sheila if she'd seen Cecelia Burke.

***

Donald wasn't much help putting up the hearts and other Valentine's Day decorations. He merely held the ladder and handed Alicia the items and pieces of tape when she asked for them. As she hung and attached everything, he kept glancing at his cell phone.

"You know you're not much of an assistant on this project."

"I didn't go to library school to learn how to put up decorations."

"Well, neither did I, Donald. Could you at least place that large heart over the door? I can hardly reach it even on the top rung of this ladder, and you're quite a few inches taller than me."

He sighed. "A helpless woman."

As Alicia stepped back down the ladder, she glared at him. "I know you do all the cooking and shopping at your house, but I bet Roger's the one who does all the heavy work. You look like you couldn't even change a flat, and even I can do that."

"You're right that Roger fixes everything, but only because we have an agreement. I'm totally capable of hard work." He got up on the ladder, and Alicia handed him the heart with a few pieces of tape affixed to the back. As he reached across to place it in the spot Alicia indicated, the ladder began to wobble under him. Alicia was tempted to let it go, but she didn't want any accidents on library property.

"You okay up there?"

"Perfectly fine, thank you. The heart is up. Happy?"

Alicia gazed up at the crooked heart. "It's lopsided, Don. It should be more to the left."

Donald held up his hands in mock frustration. "Women," he muttered. "Always perfectionists." He moved the heart an inch to the left. "What about that?"

Alicia laughed. "Now it's too much to the left."

"Don't be funny. If it's not good enough for you, you go up there and fix it." He climbed back down.

Alicia regretted not letting the ladder go earlier.

Just then, Nancy walked by. "Oh, my," she said. "That heart is lopsided. Let me fix it." Without a word, she climbed atop the ladder and perfectly adjusted the heart.

Donald threw up his hands again. "I'm outta here. You ladies take over the world."

***

A few minutes later, as Gladys took the ladder away and Donald and Alicia returned to the desk, Gilly rolled up with a hand truck full of books wrapped in Valentine-themed paper. "This was rather fun," she said. "and I only got one paper cut and grabbed one of the bodice rippers for myself."

"Looks like we're almost set. I placed the food and cake orders with the deli and bakery." Nancy looked as if she was marking off a checklist in her head. Alicia found her efficiency somewhat daunting, but she liked the public relations director and thought Sheila had chosen wisely.

It was then that Sheila returned to survey their work. "Good job, everyone," she said, looking at the decorations and the Blind Date Valentine books that Gilly had arranged on a cart near the library's entrance. She then turned to Gilly. "Laura needs some help in the Children's Room for a little while. Can you please give her a hand? I'll watch the Circulation desk."

"Sure, Sheila." Gilly headed toward the other side of the library. As soon as she'd disappeared down the ramp that led to the children's area, Sheila said, "I asked Laura to keep Gilly busy while we discuss her and Ron's party. After we close tomorrow, we'll have to add some other decorations. Nancy's designed a beautiful banner that can go across the doorway."

Donald made a face. "More decorations? My back is killing me."

"From doing what, Donald? All you did was pass me stuff, and you couldn't even hang that big heart properly."

"Now, now," Sheila said, as if seeking to get the attention of quibbling children. "I have a task more suited for Donald this time. When we set up the party upstairs, I'd like him to be in charge of the romantic music."

Donald's eyes lit up behind his glasses. "That's awesome, Sheila. You know I did a stint as a DJ back in college. I can make up a great mix. I'll do it tonight. Roger will help, too. He's excited about the party. I know you said we could bring guests."

"Of course. I'm sure you'll both do a wonderful job."

Alicia took the opportunity of Sheila being around to ask her what she'd meant to earlier. "Sheila, did you see that lady who was asking for you yesterday? I didn't see her today, but I was wondering if she came back."

"What lady?" Sheila looked puzzled.

"Mrs. Burke. She's a widow who's been visiting small towns and wanted to meet the library's director. She seemed quite impressed with our collection."

"Hmmm. I would've liked to meet her. Next time she's around, please bring her to my office."

Alicia didn't want to point out that the last time Cecelia Burke was there Sheila had been behind closed doors with Ryan Anderson.

"I can mention that you'd like to meet her," Gilly put in. "She's staying at my inn. Nice lady. Likes to knit."

"Madame Defarge," Donald muttered.

"What was that?"

"It's just a nickname Donald gave her. Gerry called her that, too," Alicia explained. "You know from *Tale of Two Cities*? I'm sure she's nothing like that character."

"You never know," Gilly said. "Sneaky didn't take a liking to her at all, and cats are good judges of characters, but she's been nothing but a perfect guest."

"I think Sneaky was just upset over his encounter with KittyKai," Alicia said.

"That wasn't a pleasant surprise for him." Gilly waved her hands. "I'm betting they'll be best of friends once they get used to one another. You need to bring him by more often."

"When did they meet?" Sheila asked, and Alicia realized she wasn't aware of her sneaking Sneaky out of the library the previous day.

Gilly had a reply ready. "I asked Alicia to bring Sneaky to the inn when I got back. I hope that was okay with you. She had him back here before the library opened."

Sheila smiled. "You know I don't consider Sneaky my cat. If he belongs to anyone, it's Alicia and maybe Laura. I have an idea, though. What if I take Sneaky to the inn tonight? He can see KittyKai again, and if Mrs. Burke is around, I can meet her."

"That would be great," Gilly said. "Like killing two birds with one stone."

"I hate that saying," Sheila said.

Donald muttered again, "Madame Defarge."

Chapter Nine

Sheila told Gilly she'd bring Sneaky to the inn on her way home. Gilly suggested they have dinner together. She asked Alicia to come and bring John and their kids, as well. Seeing Donald's pout, she offered him an invitation, too, but he declined, saying he was taking Roger out for an early Valentine's dinner at La Bella, and he was in no rush to meet Madame Defarge, anyway. Nancy said she wouldn't be able to make it, either.

Since Gilly only worked part time at the library so she could have time to manage the inn, she left at lunchtime. The rest of the day passed quickly. Before Alicia knew it, she was headed home. She'd already called John and told him not to cook dinner. He made a mock sound of disappointment, although she was sure he welcomed the break. As much as he liked to cook and was good at it, there were times he enjoyed having someone else do the job. She was happy to help on weekends, but when she worked, she was glad for him to take over the chore.

Carol and Johnny were excited to be going back to the inn. "Sneaky," Carol said as Alicia changed her into a plaid jumper and white stockings.

"Yes, Sneaky will be there, honey. So will the new kitty."

"KitKi," she said, trying to pronounce KittyKai's name.

John put the twins in the car, securing them in their car seats. Alicia got in beside him. If it were warmer, they could've walked the short distance to the Cobble Cove Inn. Alicia recalled when she first met John there when Dora ran the place. It seemed like ages ago but was only two years since her friend who'd retired to Florida had been the innkeeper.

When they pulled up to the inn, Alicia admired the red hearts and other decorations hanging outside. She hadn't paid that much attention the day before when she was in a hurry to visit and then get to work. She assumed Edith and Rose had helped put up the seasonal items. The sisters were as handy as Nancy with color and design. The interior was even nicer. Splashes of red, pink, white, and purple created a lovely atmosphere for guests. Gilly greeted them with Ruby at her side and took their coats which she hung in the hall closet that she used for the family's items. Sheila had not yet arrived. Gilly told them the sheriff was working late, and her boys had come home from school, grabbed some snacks, and then raced off to playdates with their friends. Edith and Rose wouldn't be joining them either. They'd left for the day. Now that Gilly and Ramsay were back from their honeymoon, they were no longer staying there to watch the three boys.

"Where's KittyKai?" Alicia asked as Gilly invited her and John to sit in the dining room and pulled out the fold-up high chairs she kept on hand for Carol and Johnny. The table was already set with heart-shaped white plates, red napkins, and two red candles in crystal holders at either end.

"I'm keeping her upstairs in my room until Sheila gets here with Sneaky. I want to reintroduce them. Fingers crossed they'll feel more comfortable around one another the second time they meet."

"What about Mrs. Burke? Is she in her room?" Alicia knew Sheila was coming to meet the woman who'd complimented the library and asked to see the director.

Gilly paused. "No. She's not here. She had an appointment. I know Sheila will be disappointed. She didn't say anything earlier, so I assumed she would be dining with us. She's eaten here every night so far. But when I mentioned that the library director was coming and was looking forward to meeting her, she said she was sorry but had some other plans for tonight."

"Hmmm," John said, "That's too bad. At least Sneaky will get another chance to make friends with KittyKai, and I'm looking forward to that delicious smelling food you're making." He sniffed the air. Alicia's stomach had already begun to rumble from the garlic and onion odors emanating from the kitchen.

Sheila arrived a few minutes later. She was carrying a bottle of red wine in one hand and Sneaky's carrier in the other. Gilly took the bottle from her, and Sheila placed the carrier by the couch in the inn's sitting room as Gilly instructed.

"Thank you for the wine, Sheila. I'm going to bring KittyKai in here while we eat. Don't worry, I'll keep an eye on them. We'll keep Sneaky in his box and see if KittyKai stays in the room. When we're done with dinner, I'll release Sneaky and watch from a distance how they interact."

"Sounds like Laura's been giving you training in introducing cats," Alicia said. She knew the children's librarian had experience from her volunteer work with a cat rescue shelter in Carlsville.

"I did ask her for a tip or two," Gilly admitted.

"Where's Mrs. Burke?" Sheila asked as Gilly went to retrieve KittyKai from upstairs.

"Gilly said she had a last-minute appointment tonight so won't be dining with us."

Sheila shrugged. "Oh, well. I'm sure we'll meet up another time."

"How's Professor Ryan?" John asked as they took seats in the kitchen to wait for Gilly. He preferred to call him by his title and first name.

Sheila tossed back her hair, and Johnny seated in the high chair close by, reached out to grab it. She ducked before he could get a strand between his chubby fingers. Carol was too busy peeking into the other room. "Sneaky?" she asked, fidgeting in her chair.

"We'll go see him after dinner."

"Kitki?"

"Yes, honey. We'll see KittyKai, too."

Sheila folded one of the red cloth napkins on her lap. "Ryan's fine. He said he would've come along tonight, but he was busy planning a surprise for me tomorrow. He's such a tease." She laughed. "I think he's going to bring me a gift at the library's Valentine party."

Alicia wondered why Ryan wasn't staying at the inn during his visit from California. She knew he'd booked a room at the hotel in Carlsville where the drama after the library murder last September had taken place.

When Gilly returned, she was grinning. "KittyKai is sniffing Sneaky through the carrier, and Sneaky isn't making a sound. Those are all good signs. I think they'll be ready to meet face to face after we eat." Alicia offered to help her bring out the food and joined her in the kitchen.

"Everything's already set, Alicia. I'm just bringing out the large bowl of pasta, and you can carry the sauce server if you'd like." She placed tongs in the spaghetti. "Everyone can serve themselves. I know John likes to cut up the spaghetti for your kids."

"The sauce smells delicious," Alicia said as she picked up the metal server. "Don't tell John, but this smells better than his."

Gilly winked. "Thanks, sweetie. I've been taking online cooking lessons. I've always been a baker, but I wanted to improve my culinary skills because, you know what they say the way to a man's heart is."

Alicia smiled. "You already have Ramsay's heart, and John is the one who cooks most meals in our family."

"I bet he wouldn't mind if you dished out a few tasty recipes. I could give you the link to the site."

"No thanks, Gilly. John enjoys cooking. He uses many of his mother's recipes. It's a way that helps him remember her, and Mac shared many of his own special dishes with him, too."

"Alright, but if you change your mind, it might help you spice up your kitchen, if you know what I mean?"

"Gilly!" Alicia had an urge to punch her, but she didn't want to drop the sauce bowl.

***

Dinner turned out well with John telling his usual round of jokes, and Gilly jumping in with a few off-color remarks that Alicia was glad the kids couldn't yet understand. The dessert was a delicious chocolate lava cake that Sheila said should've been saved for the following day's party. Gilly smiled her Cheshire cat grin and explained that she had thought of that and made two.

The get together moved to the sitting room where KittyKai sat directly in front of Sneaky's carrier peering in at the Siamese.

"I think they're ready," Gilly announced, opening Sneaky's box and stepping back.

Carol and Johnny started to rush forward, but Alicia stopped them. "Not yet. You'll get to pet the kitties later. I promise."

John smiled. "If they're both alive."

"Stop that!" Alicia admonished him. She sometimes felt that she had three children, but she preferred John's cocky sense of humor to the dark moods he occasionally exhibited.

KittyKai stayed still and quiet, her tail down but slowly moving back and forth like a brown pendulum.

"She's cautious but not defensive," Gilly said. "That's good. Now it's up to Sneaky."

Alicia felt like she was holding her breath as Sneaky's head slowly emerged from the carrier followed by two dark paws.

"Shhh," Gilly warned. "He's coming out. Be quiet."

Alicia knew her daughter and son were bursting to grab the cats, but she kept a steady arm on Carol while John held firm to Johnny.

When Sneaky was fully out, he and KittyKai gazed upon one another. They looked as if they were preparing to pounce on a mouse. Then Sneaky started circling KittyKai and sniffing her.

Gilly beamed like a proud mother. "They're checking each other out. This is great."

A few minutes later, Sneaky walked away from KittyKai and jumped up on Gilly's sofa in the favorite spot he usually chose when he visited the inn. Gilly didn't object because she had covers to protect the furniture.

"Why is he ignoring KittyKai now?" Alicia asked.

Gilly picked the kitten up. "I think they've made peace with one another. They'll need more time to become better acquainted. For now, being in the same room and not fighting is a breakthrough."

Carol and Johnny, no longer able to contain themselves, broke free of Alicia and John and ran to Gilly. "Pet kitty?" Carol asked. Johnny put out his splayed fingers.

"Sure you can." Gilly smiled and led the kids to the couch where she plopped KittyKai on her lap. Sneaky looked on as Carol and Johnny took turns petting KittyKai.

"Don't leave Sneaky out," Gilly said. "Otherwise, he'll be jealous."

"Love Sneaky," Carol said. After she finished with KittyKai, she patted Sneaky's head. "Kitki liberry?" she asked. Gilly looked toward Sheila. "What do you think? I wouldn't mind bringing KittyKai to the next Sneaky

Storytime, and it'll give him more of a chance to get to know her."

Sheila shrugged. "Why not? I'm sure Laura will be thrilled. Kittens can sometimes be a little wild, but KittyKai seems pretty calm."

"As calm as the beach on which I found her," Gilly said.

At her words, KittyKai suddenly jumped from her lap and began racing around the room.

John laughed. "It looks like there might've been some waves around that beach."

Carol and Johnny giggled. Alicia had to restrain them again from running after the kitten.

***

The evening ended when KittyKai fell asleep after a few laps around the room. She curled up on the couch not far from Sneaky.

"Aw. Look at them," Gilly said. "Can Sneaky stay? I'll bring him back to the library tomorrow when I come to work."

"That's a good idea," Sheila said. "I was going to ask Alicia to take him home, but there's no sense in moving him since he seems pretty comfortable here."

"Wake up, Kitki," Carol said, trying to rouse Sneaky. Alicia held her back. "No, honey. Sneaky can sleep over with us another time." She knew her children enjoyed having Sneaky at their house during the Christmas holidays when the library was closed for a few days. Alicia let the kids say goodbye to the cats without disturbing them, and Gilly walked them to the inn door.

"See you tomorrow," she said. "I hope you all enjoyed dinner."

John patted his stomach. "Sure did. Compliments to the chef."

Gilly whispered in Alicia's ear. "I'll be emailing you those cooking school links."

***

Alicia and John's car was parked next to Sheila's. As they walked to their cars, Sheila exclaimed, "Oh, no. It looks like I have a flat."

John had just finished buckling Carol and Johnny into their car seats. He and Alicia went over to Sheila. Her front right tire was flush to the ground.

"Do you have a spare?" John asked.

"Yes. In my trunk, but I don't understand. I just had the car inspected, and it's been running fine."

"You might've gone over a nail or something. I'll help you change it."

Alicia waited while John assisted Sheila. The kids looked on wide eyed as if they were part of an adventure. She marveled how they found the most uninteresting things fun.

"Thanks, John," Sheila said when the spare was in place and the flat tire in her trunk.

"That's just a donut, Sheila. You'll need to get another tire."

"I know, John. I'll go to the gas station tomorrow. I should make it home on this."

"Yes, you'll be fine." He turned to Alicia and the kids who were staring at him.

John smiled. "Okay, guys. We're going home."

As Sheila pulled away and John got in the driver's seat, he said to Alicia, "That wasn't a regular flat. Someone punctured her tire."

"Are you sure?" Alicia asked. She couldn't believe someone would deliberately damage Sheila's tire but then she thought of Mrs. Kleisman. When John nodded, she said, "It has to be that patron who threatened her. You should've told her. She could've reported it to Ramsay."

"I didn't want to upset her. For all we know, it could've been some kid fooling around."

"Then why only her tire? Our car and Gilly's were in the lot, too." Alicia recalled John coming to the same conclusion when they'd found their Christmas lights cut and how he'd turned out to be wrong.

"I don't know, Ali. I hope you're not right. When Sheila goes to the gas station, they might say something. I hate to think she has a stalker."

Alicia shuddered at the memory of being followed and the man in the trench coat standing outside a shop in Cobble Corner who'd eyed her last Christmas. "I think we should tell Ramsay."

"Maybe, but not tonight or tomorrow. Let's not ruin Valentine's Day for anyone."

They were pulling up at their house. Carol and Johnny had fallen asleep in the back seat as they often did while traveling in a car.

"Okay, John, but I'm worried about the library party. What if Mrs. Kleisman decides to turn up there and make trouble?"

"She's been banned, Ali. We'll just call the police."

Alicia got out of the car and opened the back passenger door. John helped her carry the sleeping children inside. She wasn't happy with her husband's wait and see attitude. Having experienced several crimes since moving to Cobble Cove, she'd become more cautious in her reactions to unusual events. They put the kids to bed gently, so as not to wake them. They were lucky that the twins were both sound sleepers.

"Want to work on the book tonight?" John asked as they tiptoed out of the nursery.

"I'm not in the mood. Can we just sit and talk a bit?"

"Sure. I'll go put on some tea." John knew Alicia liked a cup of herbal tea at night.

John fixed Alicia's tea the way she liked it—one lump of sugar, no milk—and poured himself a glass of sherry. He brought the drinks to the living room where Alicia sat watching the fire from the electric fireplace that she'd turned on. He handed her the cup of tea and sat next to her in the opposite rocking chair. "So, Ali, what's on your mind besides Sheila's flat?"

"I'm excited about the party. I hope it runs smoothly."

"You shouldn't worry. From what you've told me, Sheila and Nancy have everything under control. I also doubt you'll have any problems from that Kleisman woman. She sounds like she's all bark and no bite."

"I hope so."

"People like that just like to talk. You'll see. Now I have something to give you, Mrs. McKinney."

"You what?" Alicia hadn't expected John to reach in his pocket and withdraw a small jewelry box.

"I know I'm a little early, but you'll be busy tomorrow. I have reservations for us for dinner at La Palma on Saturday, but I wanted to give this to you before then."

"John. When did you . . .?"

"I had Dad and Betty watch the kids one day while you were at the library and picked it up. I hope you like it."

Alicia took the box and slipped it open. A silver locket lay nestled in the white satin lining. She gazed at the delicate flower etched on it. "Oh, John, how lovely."

"I know you wear the other one a lot, and I thought you might like one in silver. You are a locket lady after all." He grinned.

Alicia recalled when they'd traveled to New York City last year during the holidays and come upon a small shop where the proprietor had told them a wonderful story and chosen a special locket that had the verse to the Serenity Prayer. John had purchased it and kept it a surprise until he gave it to her on Christmas. "I wonder how Mr. Tinker is doing?" she said as she slipped the locket on.

"Maybe we could take another trip over a weekend and visit him," John suggested. "Not a second honeymoon this time, although I never get sick of honeymoons." He winked.

"Let's do that when the weather is warmer. I loved seeing New York in winter, but the spring is delightful."

"Not as delightful as in Cobble Cove, but, yes, we'll make a date."

"While we're exchanging, John. Would you like your gift?

"Sure." He nodded his assent.

Alicia hoped her husband would like the personalized mug she'd found in a gift catalog and had hidden away when it arrived in the mail. The mug featured a photo of her and the kids along with the cover of their first book and his name. When she gave it to him, he turned it around to view everything. "This is amazing, Ali. Every time I look at it, I'll think of you, Carol, and Johnny and the joy you've brought into my life."

She smiled. "I'm glad you like it. It's dishwasher and microwave safe, too."

"Perhaps I should store pens in it instead of drinking from it."

"Up to you. It would look good sitting on your new desk." Although John did most of his writing in bed with his laptop, they'd recently purchased a second desk for the room that Alicia used as her office.

"Great idea. Now, Mrs. McKinney, I have something else for you."

"Another gift?"

John's smile widened showing his dimple. "You might consider it that." He came over to her and planted a light kiss on her lips. "I'll save the bigger ones for upstairs."

They sat awhile after that and talked and then went up to bed where John kept his word.

Chapter Ten

The next day was Valentine's Day. Alicia usually woke before John. This morning, however, when Alicia opened her eyes, John's covers were pulled aside.

She got out of bed and checked the twins' room to make sure everything was okay, but they were sound asleep, two angels in their big kid twin beds that had recently replaced their cribs. Then she smelled it, the aroma of cooking food. She followed the scent to the kitchen where John stood over the stove flipping heart-shaped pancakes.

"You ruined it," he said with a mock frown. "I wanted to serve you breakfast in bed."

Alicia smiled. "I'll go back to bed if you'd like. Maybe we can cook up something else to do there, too. After all, the twins aren't up yet. I checked. They're sound asleep."

John almost dropped his spatula. "I like that idea, Mrs. McKinney."

But before they could leave the kitchen, they heard the clattering of tiny footsteps scrambling down the stairs.

"Mommy, Daddy," Carol said, standing in the doorway in her pink kitten pajamas complete with ears and paws. "Pancwakes."

Johnny, a few steps behind in his blue train pj's, joined her. He licked his lips.

John laughed. "Rain date for us, Mommy. Have a seat, kids. I made heart-shaped pancakes because today is Valentine's Day."

After the family ate breakfast, Alicia kissed the twins and prepared for work. She was looking forward to the patron Valentine's Day party followed by the staff party that would not only celebrate the holiday but Gilly and

Ramsay's impromptu wedding. The only thing that put a damper on her spirits was her memory of Sheila's punctured tire. She hoped the person responsible wasn't planning to do anything further to ruin the day.

"Well, see you at the library later," Alicia told John, planting a goodbye kiss on his lips.

"I'll be there as soon as Dad and Betty come to babysit." He pulled her close and whispered, "And if they're asleep when we get home, I'll take you up on your previous suggestion."

She smiled, knowing that her father-in-law's girlfriend's choral experience helped her produce the loveliest lullabies that put Carol and Johnny into a deep slumber.

"See you then," she said. Her concerns had lightened at the touch of John's lips and his promise for after the party.

***

When Alicia arrived at work, she was relieved to see Sheila's car in the director's parking spot. Nancy was also in, already making last-minute adjustments to the decorations. She wore a smart red suit with a pink scarf bursting with hearts.

"Good morning, Nancy," Alicia said as she entered the library.

Nancy greeted her with her usual bright smile. "Happy Valentine's Day, Alicia. Help yourself to a donut or some cookies." She indicated a long buffet table that held pink glazed Dunkin Donuts and a small box of munchkins. Assorted herbal tea bags lay in a white ceramic heart-shaped dish. Next to them was a carafe of hot water and one of coffee. There was also a silver tray of sugar cookies.

Sheila approached and grabbed a cookie. Munching into it, she said, "Everything looks great. Gladys wasn't too happy about having food in the main part of the library because of the cleanup, but it's not every day we have a party for the patrons."

"Are those from the bakery or homemade?" Alicia asked.

"Gilly brought these. She's coming in later today but dropped them off along with Sneaky. She'll be bringing other cookies for the staff party and that delicious chocolate lava cake she served us yesterday."

"I picked up the donuts," Nancy said. "I'm sure Ramsay will enjoy the gesture."

Alicia laughed. She knew that Gilly's husband, despite his continuing dieting efforts, had a problem saying no to donuts.

Donald walked in then wearing a heart-covered tie. "Morning, ladies." He picked up a munchkin. "These are for staff, too?"

"Sure," Nancy said. "But don't clear the table."

He grinned. "Quite a crowd out there, Nancy. I guess your advertising paid off. I haven't seen those many patrons waiting to get in since we had Alicia and John's book signing party."

Alicia's memory of that event wasn't pleasant, but she was glad people had responded to the full-page announcement in the *Cobble Cove Courier* about the library's Valentine party.

"I hope Kleisman isn't hiding in the queue," Donald added.

"Don't worry. Gerry's been assigned crowd control," Sheila assured him.

Looking through the windows, Alicia saw the security guard standing in front of the crowd, waving them back.

"Why are they so excited? Is it just the free food?"

Nancy smiled. "No, Alicia. We're doing some raffles, too. Your books are in one, and we had some donations from a few shops in Cobble Corner. Also, don't forget that we're doing the Blind Date with a Book." She pointed toward the red-clothed table adjacent to the Reference Desk that held wrapped books in a variety of Valentine prints. A sign affixed to the table with heart-shaped O's read, "Blind Date with a Book. Take one of these to bed, the park, or the beach."

"Lol," Donald said. "I bet Gilly came up with that slogan."

"She did, and I like it," Nancy said.

"I think we're ready to open." Sheila stepped forward and signaled to Gladys who'd just come in from the staff entrance. She took a key from her pocket and walked through the turnstiles to open the outside library doors.

***

The morning was busy with patrons checking out the blind date books and the romance novels Gilly had put on display in the racks at the front of the library. Bonnie, who'd recently been promoted to full time circulation clerk, had her hands full moving the line at her desk along.

Adele Wexler, the mystery lover, approached Alicia in her wide-brimmed hat. Peering through the eyeglasses that hung on a chain from her neck, she said, "I'm looking for romantic suspense. I can't read straight romance. It's too gushy for me."

Alicia brought her down the fiction aisle and showed her some of the gothics she enjoyed when she was young that were written by Phyllis Whitney, Victoria Holt, and Mary Stewart. "I think you'll enjoy these, Mrs. Wexler."

"Oh, yes," she smiled, taking a few books off the shelf. "I've read quite a few of these authors as well as Nora Roberts who's more contemporary. By the way..." She lowered her voice and turned to Alicia. "Who is that handsome older gentleman who keeps coming by and talking to Mrs. Whitehead?"

Alicia didn't like gossiping with patrons, so she replied with just the basic facts about Ryan. "He's a visiting professor from California here to do some research that Mrs. Whitehead is assisting him with."

"Hmmm. Interesting." Alicia was glad Mrs. Wexler didn't question her further but continued reading the back covers of the books she'd chosen from the stacks.

Gilly arrived after lunch and restacked some of the books that had circulated on the display. "Wow! Looks like these went quick," she commented. "As did the blind date books. Should I find some more and wrap them?" She directed the question at Nancy, who'd added some chocolate kisses to the buffet table, a handful of which Donald promptly grabbed.

"That would be great, Gilly. I have more paper upstairs. We can work on that together when you choose the books."

It was after Gilly went with Nancy to her office that Gerry came in from his post in the lobby. "Where's Sheila?" he asked Alicia. He seemed nervous about something.

"She's in her office. I think she's getting some things ready for the staff party later. Why? Is something wrong?"

"Look outside."

Alicia followed him to the library entrance. Mrs. Kleisman stood there holding a tote bag.

"She's not allowed on library property," Alicia said. "We should call the police."

"No. Wait. She told me she's here to apologize to Sheila. She brought a cake. It's in her bag. What should I do?"

"I'll go get Sheila. Keep her outside."

Alicia knocked on Sheila's door which was uncharacteristically closed. While she waited, she heard the rustle of paper from the room across the hall and Gilly and Nancy's voices as they wrapped the replacement date books.

Sheila answered before she could knock twice. "Alicia. What's the matter?"

Alicia hadn't seen the director since earlier in the day. She noticed that she now wore a pretty mauve skirt set and, rather than her usual knee-length boots, black heels showed off her long legs. Her auburn hair was tied back with a glittery headband studded with rhinestones, and her green eyes were bright. Behind her on her desk, Alicia spotted a large box wrapped in hearts. She imagined it was a Valentine's gift for Ryan.

"Mrs. Kleisman is outside, Sheila. Gerry says she wants to apologize to you and brought a cake as a peace offering."

Sheila raised a red eyebrow. Her expression changed from excitement to anger. "Is that so? After what that woman did, I don't want anything from her."

"Maybe you should hear what she has to say." Alicia didn't believe in holding grudges and hoped she'd been wrong about Mrs. Kleisman.

"You're right, Alicia. I'll do that. Tell Gerry I'll meet her in the lobby. I'll be right down. Thank you."

***

Gerry went with Sheila to speak with Mrs. Kleisman in the lobby. Alicia didn't want to be conspicuous as she watched them, so she pretended to look through the new blind date books Gilly had added to the rack by the entrance. She knew her co-workers were looking on, too. Donald had one eye on his computer screen and the other toward Sheila and Mrs. Kleisman. Gilly and Nancy were chatting, but she saw they kept glancing in the two women's direction.

Their voices were low, but Alicia tried to read the sign language between them as Sheila waved her hands animatedly. She feared one of her numerous rings would fly off. Mrs. Kleisman spoke a bit louder. "I'm sorry for how I behaved, Mrs. Whitehead, and I hope I didn't ruin your suit. I'm also ashamed about the things I said about your boyfriend. I don't blame him for how he acted."

Now Sheila's voice rose. "He's not my boyfriend, Mrs. Kleisman. We're working together on a research project." Alicia saw Gilly smile at that.

"No matter. I was wrong. Will you please accept this cake I baked for your Valentine's Day party? I'm also prepared to pay my fines if you let me use your wonderful library again."

Donald snickered behind the desk, and Alicia knew it was from the words Mrs. Kleisman spoke and not what he was watching on YouTube. Gerry, standing a few feet away from the two women, didn't look convinced of her sincerity either.

"I accept your apology," Sheila said. "You can pay at the circulation desk. We have a table set up inside for patron refreshments if you want to add your cake there."

Mrs. Kleisman smiled, and Alicia, despite Donald and Gerry's doubts, thought her expression appeared genuine. The woman followed Sheila into the library. Gerry kept a few paces behind them as if expecting Mrs. Kleisman to take a gun from her tote bag and shoot Sheila. Instead, she removed a heart-shaped chocolate cake from it that she placed on the buffet table. The cake had been stored inside a cake carrier that also doubled as a server. "You can keep the carrier until I come back," she told Sheila. "As you know, I'm an avid library user and am glad I can continue to be so. Thank you for accepting my apology."

Before Sheila could comment, she walked up to the circulation desk, took her wallet from the tote bag, and handed Bonnie several bills. "I hope this covers my fines."

Bonnie tapped some keys on her computer. "Yes, that's the exact amount, Mrs. Kleisman. Your record is now clear. Thanks for paying for the damaged books."

The woman nodded. "I'll be more careful in the future."

As she turned to leave, Sheila said, "Why don't you stay a little longer, Mrs. Kleisman? You might be interested in some of the romance books on display or the blind date ones. Also, help yourself to anything on the buffet table."

Mrs. Kleisman said, "Thank you, but I must run. I have to attend one of my kids' play at school today." As she walked out, she called over her shoulder, "I hope you enjoy the cake."

When she was gone, Sheila caught everyone staring at her. "What are you all looking at? You have to remember that our jobs in the library are serving patrons."

"I know what I'd like to serve her," Donald muttered, "and I definitely wouldn't touch that cake."

Gilly tapped him on the arm. "Why would you? You've already eaten half of what's on that table."

***

The rest of the day was uneventful. Several patrons took slices of Mrs. Kleisman's cake, so it seemed it was perfectly fine despite Donald's fears. After he'd watched them eat, he left the desk and cut himself a piece, too.

"Save up your appetite for the staff party," Nancy said. "We have lots more food coming in, and don't forget that you're in charge of the music."

"I have everything ready. I made a mix tape of love songs. Are we setting up right after we close?"

"Yes. We told the spouses and friends to arrive at 6, so we would have time to prepare everything. Some staff members are going home to change. You're picking up more cookies and your lava cake and coming back with Ron, right, Gilly?"

"Yes. I'm hoping he doesn't run too late at the station."

Alicia knew that's exactly what they wanted because they planned to surprise Gilly and Ramsay. John, Roger, Ryan, and the other non-employees who had been invited to the party were told to be there no later than a quarter to six.

As the clock struck five and the last-minute patrons exited the turnstiles, Alicia noticed Mrs. Burke slip out the door. *How strange*, she thought. *Why hadn't the old woman asked to see Sheila when she'd previously seemed so interested in meeting her?*

Chapter Eleven

As soon as the doors closed, Nancy gave out instructions. The staff members who were staying to set up were told to go upstairs to the staff lounge and decorate and put out food. Sheila and Alicia were to stay downstairs to clear off the buffet table, do some additional decorating, and welcome guests as they arrived. They were also asked to alert Nancy and the others when Gilly and Ramsay walked through the door.

When the party helpers had gone upstairs, Nancy went to the supply cabinet and removed the banner she'd created. It was composed of two huge red hearts. In the center of each, handwritten in glittery purple script, were the names of Alicia's best friend and her new husband—Gilly and Ron. Alicia knew Gilly would be glad they used her nickname but wasn't sure the sheriff would approve of the use of his first name. Most of the town's residents knew him as Ramsay.

"I'll hang this upstairs, but there are a few other decorations around that you two can add to the ones already up," Nancy said. "We don't want the Sheriff and Mrs. Ramsay to suspect anything until they get to the break room."

"You did an excellent job," Sheila said, beginning to clear off the buffet table. Alicia joined her. "Do you think any of this food can be salvaged?" A few of Gilly's muffins and some chocolate kisses were left, but only one slice of Mrs. Kleisman's cake remained. Either the woman was a natural baker, or she'd learned a lot from the baking books she'd taken out from the library.

"There's plenty of food upstairs," Sheila said. "You might as well dump everything. We can throw out the paper tablecloth, too, and fold the table up for Gerry to put away when he closes the place tonight."

After the table was cleared, Sheila took a broom from the closet and swept up crumbs on the floor. "People can be such pigs, but I have a feeling some of these were made by Donald."

Alicia laughed. She was sure Sheila was right. "Too bad Gladys went home. She could've helped us with the cleaning."

"She had to go home to feed her cats and change. I believe she's bringing a date."

Gladys had been working for the library since before Alicia came to Cobble Cove, but she still didn't know much about her background. Donald once told Alicia that the custodian was divorced with no children and not interested in marrying again.

"What did you think of Mrs. Kleisman coming by today to apologize?" Alicia asked her boss, changing the subject to one that was still on her mind.

Sheila shrugged. "I like to think the best of people. Perhaps she's turning over a new leaf."

Alicia thought of Ramsay's transformation from rude cop to friendly sheriff and nodded. "I hope so."

Nancy came back a few minutes later and admired their work. "Things are looking good upstairs. Donald is playing his music already. Roger told him he'll be here in a few minutes."

Alicia heard Air Supply's rendition of "Lost in Love" that was floating down the stairs. She wondered what other tunes Donald had chosen for his Valentine song mix tape and if the noise was bothering Sneaky in the room next door.

***

Nancy went back upstairs, and Alicia had taken her post by the door to watch for Gilly and Ramsay when Sheila called her.

"Alicia, come with me to the Reference Desk. Nancy left a few more decorations there this morning, and maybe we can find some room for them down here."

Alicia followed Sheila back to the desk, admiring the paper hearts and flowers hanging from the library's ceilings and the red streamers that lay across the stacks. Sheila rifled through some of the additional decorations that were piled next to the reference PC. She reminded Alicia of a hen tending her chickens. "Gilly and Ramsay are going to be so surprised."

"What's this?" Sheila paused.

Alicia came over to see what had grabbed the director's attention. A velvet heart-shaped box sat by one of the computer stations. As Alicia came closer, she could see a post-it attached to it with the words, "To Sheila from your secret admirer."

Sheila smiled. "That Ryan. He knows I have a sweet tooth and am particularly fond of chocolates." She opened the lid. "My favorites. I know I should wait for the party, but these are just too appealing."

Alicia watched as Sheila took a piece. Only a few seconds after she swallowed, her smile faded. She began to choke and clutched her throat.

"Sheila, are you okay?" Alicia rushed over, trying to recall how to do the Heimlich maneuver, but Sheila had already passed out on the floor. "Help!" Alicia called, racing to the stairs. The romantic music playing above drowned out her voice. Just as she grabbed her cell phone to dial 911, Ryan Anderson walked through the door, a huge bouquet of roses in his arms. He stopped short seeing Sheila on the ground. "What happened. Oh my God!"

"I'm dialing 911 right now," Alicia said. "She ate one of your chocolates and then passed out. I'm not sure if she choked on a piece."

"My chocolates? I didn't get her any chocolates. I was bringing her these flowers." He dropped them on the desk and then knelt and started administering CPR to Sheila's unmoving body.

Chapter Twelve

Sheila was alive, but the party was ruined. They brought her to the hospital in Carlsville where John and his sister Pamela had once shared a room that terrible December two years ago. The place still gave Alicia the creeps, but then, hospitals were far from happy places unless you were going there to deliver babies.

"She was lucky," Dr. Crandall, a young doctor with his name label sewn on his white lab coat, said as he walked out to the waiting room where everyone was gathered still in their party clothes. He gave them the news that Sheila had been poisoned but would make a complete recovery after having her stomach pumped.

There was a collective sigh. Alicia cried tears of relief, and Gilly hugged her.

Ramsay, who'd arrived with his wife as Ryan was trying to revive Sheila on the library floor, said, "I already have men on this case. We'll find out who brought those chocolates into the library and made an attempt on Mrs. Whitehead's life." He glanced at Ryan who'd stopped his pacing. His white hair was ruffled from his running his fingers through it as he waited for the news. Now he stopped and faced the doctor. "May I see her?"

"I'm afraid not, sir. We're only allowing close relatives in. Are there any family members here?" The doctor scanned the group.

John, who'd entered as the ambulance had pulled up at the library and still had his arm around Alicia to offer her comfort, said, "Her daughter's in California, and her husband is dead, so there are no relatives here in Cobble Cove, but she's always been close to my family. Can you make an exception and let one of us in?"

"If anyone should go in," Nancy said from the corner by the fake evergreen plant, "It should be Alicia." Nancy had felt the weight of the incident fall on her shoulders, feeling responsible for having held the party. Donald, seated next to Roger by the window, nervously fingering his heart tie, shook his head in agreement. "Alicia and Sheila have been through a lot together. She should be allowed to see her."

"Very well, but make it quick," Dr. Crandall said. Alicia followed him down the antiseptic hall, recalling the smells that masked the odors of illness.

As she entered the room, Sheila was propped up in bed, her red hair fanned against her pillow. Her headband had been placed on the bureau next to her. Her face had a sallow tone, and she was breathing through an oxygen mask.

"Sheila," Alicia said, feeling the tears threaten again. "The doctor told us you're going to be okay, thank God."

Sheila smiled weakly. "Well, I don't feel great right now. I guess that's what I get for going off my diet with those chocolates."

Alicia tried to smile at Sheila's attempt at humor. "It's not your fault. Ramsay's going to find out who did this. You just focus on getting better."

Before Sheila could reply, a nurse came in the room to notify Alicia her time was up with the patient.

She told Sheila to rest and went back to the waiting room. As soon as John saw her, he pulled her aside. "Alicia, I talked with Dr. Crandall, and he thinks Sheila will be released tomorrow. I've also spoken with Ramsay about her tire. He thinks it was the first attempt to harm her and will be putting some men on to watch her house. He's trying to keep it quiet and doesn't even want her to know. I called Andy and instructed him not to report anything about this in the *Courier*. The library will open as usual tomorrow per Betty's orders." Betty was the president of the library's Board of Directors.

"I don't understand, John. I know Sheila will try to come back as soon as possible, but she really needs to get her strength back."

"Sheila doesn't usually work weekends. Hopefully, she'll be feeling her normal self by Monday."

Alicia glanced at the others waiting for an update on Sheila's condition. Ryan had continued his pacing, but now he held a bouquet of flowers from the hospital gift shop. Alicia imagined he hoped he would be allowed in to see her soon or one of the nurses could bring them to her.

"I better go tell everyone she's up and talking."

John put out an arm to hold her back. "One minute, Ali. There's something else." His blue eyes had darkened, and Alicia worried the doctor had told John something else about Sheila's diagnosis.

"What, John? I thought they were releasing Sheila tomorrow. She must be recovering enough for them to do that."

"It's not about Sheila. Ramsay has asked Betty to release the footage of the library security cameras to see who left that box of chocolates on the desk. The chocolates were also sent to a lab to determine what poison they were laced with. The box itself came from a shop in Cobble Corner, and Ramsay's going to check with the proprietor about who bought it. However, there's a chance the chocolates inside weren't the ones originally in the box."

"What are you saying, John?"

He brushed back a strand of dark hair tipped with gray that had fallen across his forehead. "What I'm saying is that those chocolates may have been homemade."

Alicia gasped, and the heads in the waiting room turned to look at her. "John," she whispered. "There was a patron who recently took out books on chocolate making." She was thinking of Mrs. Kleisman.

Chapter Thirteen

Things moved swiftly after that. Ryan managed to get in to see Sheila. John accompanied him. Ramsay also got in for a few minutes to question Sheila but was chased out by the nurse when Sheila's blood pressure monitor showed a spike.

When everyone was satisfied Sheila was on the road to recovery, they began to leave. Donald caught Alicia as she was heading out the door with John. "I'm glad this didn't turn out to be a second murder in the library," he said. Alicia thought that a rude comment and didn't return his laugh. Roger, at his side, said, "You should be glad your boss is okay, Don."

Gilly approached Alicia next. "Hon, do you and John mind giving me a ride back to the inn? Ron has already gone to the station. He's eager to get started on this investigation."

"No problem. We have to pass the inn, anyhow." Alicia felt awful that Gilly's surprise party had turned into a disaster. She vowed to speak with Nancy later to hold another one for her friend.

***

"When will they be checking the videotape?" Alicia asked as she sat next to John in the car. Gilly, from the back seat, said, "Betty already gave it to Ron. He'll be viewing it as soon as he gets back to the station. That's why he was in such a hurry."

"I wonder what it'll show." Alicia was thankful that this time the security cameras hadn't been disabled as they had when they'd found Mary Beth's body in the stacks.

"I have a feeling it won't be that lady you think has a vendetta against Sheila."

"I'm not sure, John, but it's odd that she apologized yesterday if she was planning to kill her."

"Exactly. The person who did this must've had a stronger motive than having to pay for damaged library books or being pushed by a protective boyfriend."

"That's not necessarily true. Some people kill for odd reasons. Who do you think's behind this?"

As he made a left toward the Cobble Inn, he said, "Me? I say it's the professor. He's the stranger around here. Maybe she's not giving him what he wants, or maybe he came to Cobble Cove for another reason."

"I'm curious about him, too," Gilly said. "You know, Alicia, maybe it's time you called Sheila's daughter in California to let her know her mother was hospitalized. You might be able to slip in some questions about Ryan."

Alicia worried that Gilly was considering working with her on their own private investigation of the person who'd poisoned Sheila. The last time they took the detecting work on themselves, they'd nearly paid for it with their lives.

"You're right. Julie should know what happened to her mother. I'll keep you posted."

When they pulled up at the inn, Alicia noticed KittyKai peeking through an upstairs window of the inn. She looked as if she'd lived there forever. She also saw Mrs. Burke sitting on the porch with her knitting and remembered she'd seen the woman leave the library right before Sheila consumed the chocolates. She wondered if the library tapes would show her sneaking to the reference desk with her knitting bag and removing a heart-shaped box from it. Then she flashed back to Sheila's tire. *Would a knitting needle make a good tool to puncture a tire?* She voiced her thought to John.

"Hmm," he considered. "A knitting needle probably wouldn't do much to a tire, but a screwdriver might and could be concealed in a knitting bag. But don't let your mind run off with you, Ali. What motive would an elderly widow have to harm Sheila?"

She acknowledged he had a point, but she still felt there was something odd about Cecelia Burke.

When they arrived home, Mac was with the twins. It looked as if they'd gotten back just in time because Johnny had grabbed Mac's cane and was running around with it, Fido tagging along and barking in accompaniment, as Carol stood giggling.

"If Betty hadn't been busy with the police, I could've used her help," Mac said as his son and daughter-in-law entered.

"Oh, no," Alicia cried. "Johnny, give your grandpa back his cane."

As usual, Johnny ignored Alicia. But when John gave him a stern look and muttered in a serious tone, "Young man, listen to your mother or you'll be punished," the boy ran back to Mac. "Sorwee, Grampa."

Mac took the cane and stood up, looking eager to leave. Fido joined him, out of breath for an old dog.

"And you, young lady," Alicia addressed Carol. "I think you were behind this." She knew from experience that Carol egged Johnny on and gave him ideas that got him into trouble.

Carol looked up at her mother innocently. "No, Mommy. We pwaying."

"Go to your rooms," John told them. When they pouted but obeyed and headed up the stairs, Mac said, "How is Sheila?"

"She'll be alright, but they're keeping her overnight," Alicia told him. "Betty called a little while ago. She went to the station with Ramsay to view the library security film. I hope it helps them find whoever did this." Mac's face was grim.

"The camera was situated right over the desk," John said, "It should've gotten a clear picture of the perpetrator. He'll be behind bars by tonight."

"Let's hope so. It's hard to believe no one saw the person who left those poisoned chocolates behind the reference desk."

"We were busy with the party," Alicia explained. "I know it's no excuse, but we were away from the desk at certain times that day."

"It's a shame it ruined things for Gilly and the sheriff. I know you all went through a lot of trouble putting it together." Mac leaned against his cane as he walked toward the door.

"They'll have something else another time," John said. "The main thing is we find out who was behind this attempt on Sheila's life. I told Ramsay about her tire being punctured at the inn last night. I should've reported it then."

"You thought it was young vandals," Alicia said, realizing as she spoke the words that this hadn't been the first time John had made the wrong conclusion about an attempted crime.

"Well, I'm heading to the hospital to see Sheila if they let me. Then I hope Betty will be home with some news."

"They wanted Sheila to rest, Dad." John met him at the door. "I've asked Andy to keep this out of the paper until the culprit is caught."

"Good idea, Son. Do you mind keeping Fido, so I can go directly to the hospital? I'll pick him up on my way back?"

"No problem," John said, bending down to pet the panting golden retriever. Alicia knew how difficult it was to keep up with toddlers. As an older mother, she often found herself out of breath chasing them and knew John had the same problem even though he kept fit with daily exercise.

***

They put the kids to bed who, thanks to their earlier activity, had fallen asleep as soon as Alicia and John had read them their last bedtime story. Tiptoeing from the nursery, John whispered, "I'm going to the office to work on our next chapter. Are you joining me?"

Alicia declined. "No, I'm a little tired, John. I want to call Sheila's daughter and then maybe read for a bit. If you need any help with the chapter, just let me know."

John hesitated. "Are you sure it's a good idea to call Julie, Ali?"

"She should know her mother was in the hospital."

"Yes, but I don't think you should tell her it was because of a murder attempt."

"I know it'll be upsetting to her, but I want to tell her the truth."

John nodded. "Whatever you think is best, but Sheila might be mad if her daughter comes running out here to protect her."

"I don't think that'll happen and, even if it does, maybe it's a good thing. It's not that I don't trust Ramsay and his men, but Sheila should have someone staying with her. She's all alone in that house."

"She's been alone for years, Ali. She's a tough lady. The toughest woman I know besides my sister."

Alicia laughed, but then she remembered how John's sister Pamela was no match for the person who shot her a year before.

"I'm just worried for her, John."

"So am I, honey." He turned and headed for the stairs.

***

Alicia went into their bedroom and took out the address book she kept in her desk drawer. It hadn't been updated in a while because most of the numbers she dialed regularly were stored in her phone. However, she'd never called Julie West. Ramsay had back when Sheila was in California, and he'd suspected her of foul play. That now seemed ages ago, when Alicia had just arrived in Cobble Cove and met John.

She flipped through to the W's: Benjamin West, Julie's husband's phone number. She decided to use the landline to place the call. Nervously, she dialed the number including the area code. She hoped she wasn't calling too early because of the three-hour time difference. It wouldn't yet be six o'clock in California. Sheila said her daughter worked until three so she could pick her kids up from school.

A woman answered the phone, the clatter of dishes and the familiar noise of young children behind her. "Hello."

"Hi. This is Alicia McKinney from Cobble Cove. Sorry to interrupt your dinner." She suddenly felt John was right that she shouldn't be calling Sheila's daughter.

"That's okay. I'm still waiting on my husband. Is everything alright, Mrs. McKinney? Are you calling about Mom?" The young woman's voice became strained, and Alicia was afraid to proceed. She took a deep breath and said, "Yes, Mrs. West. Sheila's doing okay, but she's in the hospital." Before Alicia could continue, Julie said in a high-pitched voice, "Oh, no. What happened? Was she in an accident?"

Alicia swallowed the lump that had formed in her throat. "No. Uh, she had a bit of food poisoning." She decided a half truth was better than alerting Sheila's daughter that a murder attempt had been made on her mother.

Julie let out a breath. "Can I call her? Do you have the number of the hospital?"

"I can give that to you, but they want her to rest. You might be better off calling tomorrow when she's home."

"I can do that. I'll call in the morning. Will they be releasing her by noon?"

"I'm not sure. You can try."

"Are you sure she's okay? Give me the hospital number, anyway."

Alicia recited the main hospital number. "That's the hospital's phone. She doesn't have a line set up in her room now because she's only staying overnight, but the room number is 105."

"Thank you. I really appreciate your letting me know. Mom would never tell me. She doesn't like to worry us, but we're so far away that I feel cut off from her." She spoke away from the phone. "Suzie, don't touch that yet. Your father will be here soon."

"I thought you should be notified. I know it's hard not to worry, but we're looking out for your mother here." Alicia paused, remembering that Gilly had suggested she ask about Ryan Anderson. "I don't want to keep you tied up while you're preparing dinner, but can I ask you one thing?"

"Of course. I just have two hungry kids trying to steal dinner before their dad is home."

Alicia laughed. "I know the feeling. My little ones are also eager to be fed. In my case, it's usually my husband waiting for me to come home."

"How old are your children, Alicia?"

"They'll be two this spring and advanced for their ages. They keep us busy."

"Ah, toddlers. I don't envy you. Mine are in elementary school, 2nd and 3rd grades. Great ages for kids." She paused. "What did you want to ask me?"

Alicia took advantage of their sharing about their children to approach the subject on her mind. "I'm curious about Professor Anderson. Sheila told me you were the one who recommended him to your mother for his research project."

Julie said, "Oh, yes. I've known Ryan since college. He was one of my professors at UCLA. I actually had a little crush on him." She gave a short laugh that sounded a bit embarrassed to Alicia. "I was dating Ben at the time, though, and Ryan was old enough to be my father. Of course, you know my own father died when I was very young. I hardly remember him."

"Sheila told me. It must've been hard for both of you."

"It was, but Mom was amazing. We're very close. That's why it was hard to go away to college. I've always wanted to find a way to make it up to her." Her voice dropped to almost a whisper. "That's maybe why I told Ryan to go to Cobble Cove. My mother's been a widow a long time and when I heard about Ryan's research project, I, well, I think you can put together the pieces."

"You were trying to matchmake them?"

Julie laughed again. "I guess that's the term. Ryan had a lot of girlfriends and almost married once. She had a car accident. I thought that he and my mother had similar tragedies and might find something together."

Alicia thought about her and John and how they'd both lost their spouses. "It seems they do, Julie. I hope it works out." She was now convinced Ryan had nothing to do with Sheila's poisoning.

"So do I. Thanks again, Alicia, but I think I hear Ben coming in now. I have to go. Please keep me posted about Mom. I'll call her tomorrow."

"It was nice speaking with you, Julie. You must visit us in Cobble Cove."

"Definitely. Maybe during a school break. Mom usually comes here, but it would be great to visit her there.

She's told me some great things about the town and about you."

Alicia felt a blush start at the compliment. "If it wasn't for your mother, I would never have furthered my relationship with my husband," she said, remembering Sheila's offer for her to work at the library.

"I'm sure Mom owes you a lot, too. Bye, now."

Alicia hung up, feeling positive about having made the call. Just as she hung up, her cell rang. She saw it was Gilly on the other end and thought she was calling with news about the videotape and the lab results of the chocolates.

"Hi, Gilly. What's up?"

"Ali, you're not going to believe this, but we were all wrong about who poisoned Sheila."

"What?" Alicia was confused. "Did Ramsay catch someone?"

"He's on his way to make the arrest now. The library tape was very clear."

"Hold on. You're saying the tape showed who put the chocolates on the desk and that it wasn't Ryan, Mrs. Kleisman, or Mrs. Burke."

"Nope." Alicia was growing frustrated with how her friend liked to create suspense by keeping information to herself as long as possible.

"Well, tell me, Gilly. Who did they see on the tape?"

"Kevin Tucker."

Alicia's memory flashed back to the young man who had once been suspected of selling drugs, stalking her, and kidnapping her children. He'd been cleared when the true perpetrator had been caught. Why in the world would he target Sheila?

Chapter Fourteen

After hanging up with Gilly, Alicia raced down the stairs to the office she shared with John. He was sitting at the computer typing, his face deep in concentration on their mystery novel.

"John, I'm sorry to interrupt, but I just had news from Gilly. They've found the person who put the poisonous chocolates at the reference desk, and you won't believe who it is."

John paused and turned to look at her. "That's good news, Ali. I guess it wasn't Anderson. A few of us had our money on him."

"No, it wasn't the professor. It wasn't anyone we were considering."

"Who was it then? Save this drama for our mysteries and reveal the culprit."

"It's Kevin Tucker, John. Do you remember him?"

"Andy's friend, the one who used to sell dope. He was supposed to have gone clean."

Alicia knew John was referring to how Kevin had helped recover stolen jewels that had been hocked for drug money. "It's hard to believe, John. Why in the world would he try to kill Sheila?"

John sighed. "Ali, people on drugs are capable of anything. It's too bad he got back into it. Andy will be upset."

"It doesn't seem right, though. Even if he's guilty, and I'm not saying the videotape was tampered with or anything, but why go through the trouble of poisoning chocolates? He could've just shot Sheila. Wouldn't that have been a more likely action for a man high on drugs who wanted to kill someone?"

"You've got a point, Ali, but let's leave those questions up to Ramsay when he arrests Tucker."

"How about calling Andy? I'm sure he'd want to know about this."

"That's not a good idea. Andy is still working for me at the paper. He has to be impartial about the stories he covers. If anyone should write this up for the *Courier*, it should be me." He got up from his desk chair, rolling it back as he stood. "I'm going down to the station and getting the full scoop. You stay here with the kids, Ali."

"I thought you said you were keeping Sheila's murder attempt out of the paper."

"It's different now that they've caught the person responsible. I'm glad they worked so quickly. I'd hate to think that Sheila remained in danger."

***

John returned an hour later. Alicia had stayed in the office editing some of the chapter he'd been working on. She'd had a hard time concentrating because it nagged at her that something was wrong. Even if John believed Tucker had fallen off the wagon, she was convinced the police were arresting the wrong man.

John let himself in quietly and came into the office. He didn't seem surprised to see her sitting at the desk. "It's over, Ali," he said, his face pale in the light from the desk lamp.

"They arrested Tucker?"

"Not exactly."

"What do you mean, John? Did you speak with Ramsay?"

"I did." He cast his eyes down at the floor.

She came over to him. "What's going on? What aren't you telling me?"

John lifted his head to look at his wife, his blue eyes dark and sorrowful. "Ramsay found Tucker in his car a few blocks from his house. He was dead, shot in the head. The weapon wasn't recovered."

Chapter Fifteen

Alicia had a hard time processing John's words. A memory flooded back to her of when she and John found a man shot in the *Cobble Cove Courier* office on that fateful December night when they were hunting a kidnapper. The murdered man had been their prime suspect.

"That means the person who tried to kill Sheila is still around and has a gun."

"I'm afraid so, Ali. Ramsay thinks Tucker was hired to drop off that box of chocolates. After he did his job, he had to be eliminated."

"But why in his car? Were there any witnesses?"

"Ramsay wouldn't tell me much. I'm sure he's looking into everything. When I left the station, the poor guy was munching donuts, and you know how he's trying not to fall back into unhealthy old habits."

"What do we do, John? Sheila's supposed to be going home tomorrow."

"Ramsay's keeping men on watch outside her house. I have to write the story. First, I need to call Andy. I'm not looking forward to that." He walked to his desk chair and plopped down. "Go back to bed. I'm going to be here awhile."

Alicia hesitated. She knew she wouldn't be able to sleep, but she had an idea. "Okay, but don't stay up all night." He was already reaching for the phone as she left the room.

***

Upstairs, Alicia used her cell to call Gilly. "Sorry if I'm calling too late, Gilly, but I thought I should tell you what happened tonight."

Gilly didn't sound sleepy. "Don't worry about that, Alicia. The boys are still up making a ruckus in their rooms. No school or work tomorrow, and I'm waiting for Ron."

"You may be waiting awhile. John went to the station to confirm the arrest, and Ramsay told him they found Kevin Tucker's body, shot in his car a few blocks from his house."

There was a pause on the other end of the line, and then Gilly said, "Wow! That'll make headlines tomorrow. You know what this means, don't you?"

"Yes. That Sheila's still in danger."

"It also means we've got a case."

"Gilly, no. We're not investigating on our own again." Alicia kept her voice as firm as she did when she was warning Johnny and Carol.

"Why not? We caught the killer last time."

Alicia recalled what happened at the Carlsville Holiday Inn with a shudder. "You mean, he caught us. Gilly, we were nearly killed. We need to leave the investigative work up to the sheriff and his men. Don't you trust your husband to solve this?"

"I do, but we might be able to solve it sooner. If you don't agree to work with me, I'll do it myself."

Alicia didn't want to see her friend put herself in danger. On the other hand, she had to admit she'd dialed Gilly knowing this would be her response.

"What are you planning to do?"

"Recheck the clues like we did last time. I know Ron spoke to the manager of the chocolate shop in Cobble Corner. That's where they think the chocolates were purchased. I've had a sudden craving for chocolates and thought I'd drop by the store tomorrow. Wanna come?"

Alicia couldn't believe she'd agree to this, but a strange surge of excitement ran through her at the thought.

"We're not working tomorrow. I guess I can accompany you."

"Good girl. Meet me at the inn at eleven o'clock. Maybe we can have lunch afterwards and discuss the case further. In the meantime, not a word to John, understand?"

"Yes, ma'am, and I know you won't say anything to Ramsay."

***

John came to bed a little after midnight. Alicia was still awake, reading the first of a cozy mystery series to keep her mind off things. Reading other authors who wrote in her and John's genre also helped her keep current in the field.

"You didn't have to wait up," John said as he slipped into the room. There were dark shadows around his eyes, and strands of his hair were sticking up as if he'd run his hands through them in his usual habit when he was frustrated. Alicia reflected that their son had picked up the same habit.

"I couldn't sleep, John. I decided to read. I thought it might help me relax. What about you? How did it go with Andy?"

He grabbed a pair of pajamas from the closet, walked to the bed, and began to undress. "Not well, Ali. He said Kevin was just getting his life back on track. He told me something that sort of explains why he was shot."

Alicia put down her book, being careful to bookmark the spot. "What did he tell you?"

John finished dressing and got into bed next to her. When he replied, he was looking straight ahead at their bureau. "It seems Kevin was having a hard time finding work because of his previous record, so he started his own business a few months ago. He called it Kevin's Courier Service."

"He was a courier?" Alicia started putting the pieces together.

John nodded and turned to her. "Yes. He delivered mostly to businesses in the area. Ed at the post office was peeved that he was taking some customers away from him, but he was quicker than overnight service. He also advertised in the paper, and people contacted him to have other items delivered."

"So the person who killed him hired him to bring Sheila's chocolates to the library?"

"That's what I'm thinking, but I told Andy to speak with Ramsay."

"That's so sad. I'm sure Andy is devastated."

"He is. He wants to hold a memorial service for Kevin. He had no family here in Cobble Cove and said he wanted to be cremated, but Andy wants to put something together. I'll help him."

"I hope Ramsay finds his killer and the person who's after Sheila."

"So do I, Ali. I'm planning to check on her tomorrow after she's released from the hospital. I can ask Dad to watch the kids if you want to come with me."

Alicia remembered her promise to Gilly. "Actually, I made plans to have lunch with Gilly. I'm meeting her earlier at the inn. I'll probably be back by the time Sheila's home and would be happy to go along with you."

John raised an eyebrow. "We usually do family stuff on Saturdays when you're home. When did you make these plans?"

"Sorry, John. I called Gilly while you were downstairs. Since she's been back from her honeymoon, I haven't had much of a chance to spend time with her. I hope you understand." Alicia felt guilty not revealing the true reason she was seeing her friend.

John shrugged. "I understand. Maybe I'll take the kids out in the morning to that new children's museum that opened recently. They loved it when we brought them last month."

Alicia recalled the grand opening of the Cobble Cove Children's Museum. It was geared toward young kids and had a playroom for those under five. There was another area for elementary-age children. Patty Milburn, a second grade teacher who often brought her class to story times, told Alicia she'd already booked a field trip there and was taking her daughter Angelina along too, even though she was now in third grade.

"That sounds like fun, John. I'll call you when I'm home, and maybe we can drop Johnny and Carol at Mac and Betty's house when we see Sheila."

"Good plan, Ali. Goodnight then." John flicked off the lights. Alicia wondered if he suspected she'd be discussing Kevin's murder with Gilly. It was likely he did because he knew how close the women were. Hopefully, he didn't suspect that they'd be starting their own investigation again. She'd promised him last time that she'd never do that again. As she closed her eyes to try to sleep, she was thankful that the children's museum wasn't located in Cobble Corner near Cocoa Cocoa, the chocolate shop.

Chapter Sixteen

The next day was cold but bright. Since she wasn't working, Alicia slept late. John, emotionally exhausted from writing the article on Kevin's murder and breaking the terrible news to Andy, was still asleep when Alicia rose at nine to the pitter patter of little feet and a tiny knock on her door.

Alicia opened the door to her daughter behind whom stood her son.

"Mama. Up. Hungy," Carol said.

Alicia got out of bed, leaving John to sleep. As she made pancakes, Carol stood by watching and rubbing her tummy. Johnny sat in his chair, curling his dark hair around his fingers. Their son's hair was beginning to reach below his ears, so Alicia made a note to ask John to take him to the barber's.

Carol kept by her mother's side as Alicia plugged in the electric mixer. "Don't get too close, honey," she warned. "I don't want to splatter you."

After Alicia finished mixing the batter, Carol stuck out her fingers. Alicia knew her daughter wanted a taste of the mix. "I can only give you a little bit," she said. "You don't want to ruin your appetite." Alicia put a dollop on a spoon and handed it to Carol who licked it clean. "Yummy!" she said, her eyes lighting up.

A few minutes later, Carol was back in her chair next to Johnny, and Alicia was flipping pancakes on the stove. John walked in, rubbing the sleep from his eyes.

"Daddy!" Carol yelled. "Mommy make pancwakes."

John laughed. "Looks like you tried some already." Alicia had forgotten to wipe the batter from around Carol's mouth.

"I think everyone will like these better," Alicia said as she brought a plate full of golden-brown pancakes to the table.

"Good job," John said taking a spatula and giving each of the kids a pancake. He placed another on Alicia's plate and one on his. "These look so good, and I'm starving."

Alicia gave him a kiss on the cheek. "Good morning. Did you get any sleep?"

"Not much, but I'm okay. I'm looking forward to taking the kids to the children's museum today."

Johnny, already biting into his pancake, stopped in mid chew and said, "Moozeem." His blue eyes, so like his dad's, lit up.

Carol asked, "Mommy go?"

"No, I'm afraid not, honey," Alicia said taking a seat next to her daughter. "Mommy has some things to do this morning, but I promise I'll spend all day with you tomorrow."

Carol pouted. "No like moozeem, Mommy?"

Alicia felt guilty for making plans with Gilly, some of which she'd hidden from John. "I do, sweetie, and I'll go with you another time. You'll have fun with Daddy. Then, afterwards, you'll go to Grandpa's house."

"Pway Fido?" Johnny asked. He was especially fond of Mac's old golden retriever.

"If you're gentle with him," John answered.

***

After breakfast, John helped Alicia clean up and dress the kids to go out. The museum opened at ten, so they spent some time watching cartoons in the den before Alicia took the kids' coats from the closets, and she and John helped slip their arms through the sleeves. "I guess I should bring the double stroller," John said. "They might get tired walking in the museum. It's a big place."

"Good idea."

John went upstairs to the nursery where the twin stroller was stored and carried it downstairs where Carol and Johnny were waiting impatiently to leave. He gave Alicia a kiss goodbye. "Have a nice time with Gilly," he said. Then, as he grabbed the car keys from the hook by the door, he added in a whisper, "And don't start snooping around with her into the sheriff's investigation."

Alicia knew she didn't look convincing when she replied, "Of course not, John. I made you a promise not to do that again."

***

Gilly rushed out of the inn as soon as Alicia pulled up. She wore a navy blazer over jeans and a red mock turtleneck. Alicia thought she wasn't dressed warm enough for the bitter February morning and was surprised she didn't wear the fur Ramsay had bought her.

"Good morning, Ali," she said, jumping into the passenger seat. "Edith and Rose are here today and are watching the inn and the boys, but I still don't want to stay out too long."

"I can't be out late either. John took the kids to the children's museum, but we need to drop them at Mac's place later because we want to visit Sheila when she gets home."

"I should do that, too, but maybe she shouldn't have too many visitors while she's recovering. Ron promised he'd keep men watching the place 24/7."

"She might not like that, Gilly."

"She won't know about it unless someone says something. They're keeping their distance and using unmarked cars."

"What about when she goes back to work? How are they going to protect her at the library?"

"Ron is sure that whoever tried to poison her at the library won't try it again there." Gilly shook her dark head, and Alicia noticed some of her curls had been trimmed.

"When did you have your hair cut, Gilly?" Alicia asked as she was driving toward Cobble Corner.

"I had it done in Hawaii. You probably didn't notice. It's only slightly shorter."

"Looks good and so do you, in general." Alicia had to admit marriage seemed to agree with her friend.

"It's all the sex," she said, making Alicia nearly slam on the brakes.

"Gilly! You could've gotten us killed."

"Well, what do you think newlywed couples do? Or are you and John done with the honeymoon stage?"

"We're fine, Gilly. We just don't talk about it. Some things are kept private."

"Talk about private, I wonder what we'll find out at the chocolate shop. Ron said he had them release their surveillance tapes, but Kevin Tucker wasn't on them. He also spoke with the shop's owner, Margaret Simmons, but she said the store's been so busy lately that she couldn't keep an eye on all the customers."

"Hmm." Alicia considered this information. "If Ramsay didn't have any luck, how can we expect to find anything there?"

"It's always a good idea to question witnesses more than once. Besides, I might have some new questions for Ms. Simmons."

"Gilly, I'm not happy about doing this with you. I made a promise to John, but I think he suspects I'm breaking it."

"Stop worrying, Ali. We're just conducting a citizen's investigation. I'll share everything with Ron if we find anything useful."

"That won't help if we're dead," Alicia said.

Gilly didn't reply.

***

Cocoa Cocoa was a new shop located in Cobble Corner across from the bakery. It featured delectable displays of chocolates in its windows. Alicia, a chocoholic, felt her mouth water as she and Gilly approached the store. A bell tinkled as they entered, and a tall, thin woman with long white hair wearing a red striped apron over black slacks greeted them.

"Good morning, ladies. Is there anything I can help you with? Now that Valentine's Day has passed, all boxed chocolates are on sale."

"Hello, are you the manager?" Gilly asked.

"Yes. I am. My name's Margaret Simmons."

"Nice to meet you, Margaret. I'm Gilly Nostran, and this is my friend, Alicia McKinney."

Alicia winced at Gilly's use of her maiden name. She figured she was trying to hide the fact that she was the sheriff's wife because Ramsay had already questioned Mrs. Simmons.

"A pleasure to meet you both. Are you looking for anything special today?"

Gilly glanced around the room, and Alicia caught her eyeing the assorted chocolates behind the glass counter. Beside the counter, a display of boxed candy bearing the logo 'Cocoa Cocoa,' was arranged. A sign hung from it that said, "All Valentine's Candy 50 per cent off."

"I'm curious," Gilly said. "Those boxes aren't Whitman's or Russell Stover's. Do you make your own chocolates here?"

"Yes, indeed," Mrs. Simmons said proudly. "There's nothing like homemade chocolate. We even give classes if you're interested."

Gilly's eyes lit up even wider than they were from viewing the chocolates. "Is that so? Do a lot of people take them?"

"A few. The enrollment was quite high near Valentine's Day."

Alicia knew what Gilly suspected and anticipated her next question to the chocolate shop manager. "Do you keep a list of people who take your classes?"

Simmons' smile faded. "Strange you should ask that. The sheriff was here the other day and asked me that, too."

"The sheriff?" Alicia thought Gilly could win an Emmy for her mock expression of surprise.

"Yes. He was investigating that poisoning at the library. Awful thing. Did you ladies hear about it?"

Alicia was about to say they worked there, but Gilly answered quickly. "We did. It was in the paper today. They caught the man who brought the chocolate box to the library, but someone shot him."

"Mr. Tucker. Oh, yes. Sheriff Ramsay asked me about him, but I couldn't recall seeing him lately. It's been so busy this week with the crowd of last-minute Valentine's Day chocolate buyers that I find it hard to remember any of the customers. I was shocked when Sheriff Ramsay told me what happened. What is this world coming to that such a thing would occur in a nice small town like Cobble Cove? I moved here recently to get away from the city and opened this shop. My husband and I had a store in Manhattan. He died last year, and I sold the shop to open one here. Most women my age would've moved to Florida, but I like the changing seasons and my daughter lives on the other side of town. Her husband works in New Paltz, and they settled here. No kids yet, but I'm hoping to be a grandma soon and am glad I can be nearby to lend her a hand. Now I'm worried this isn't the safest place, but I'm sure crime is everywhere today. You can't stop living your life."

Gilly nodded. "I agree, Ms. Simmons. May I call you Margaret?"

"Of course. About Thursday's chocolate class list, I gave a copy to the sheriff. Were you interested in signing up? I have another this Wednesday afternoon. I'm teaching this one. My assistant, Clara Wiggs, gave the other."

"I'm not interested in taking the class right now, but do you mind if I can see the list you copied? I'm wondering if one of my friends took the class."

Alicia was amazed Simmons didn't find this request odd, but Cocoa Cocoa's owner went to the register and reached into a drawer underneath from which she took a paper. "We had five on Thursday. Each person left with a complimentary box of candy." She handed Gilly the list.

Alicia peered over Gilly's shoulder as she read the names. There were three women and two men. She recognized none of them, but maybe Gilly did. After all, she was now the owner of the town's inn.

"I don't see my friend on this," Gilly said handing the list back to Simmons, "but thank you, Margaret."

The woman smiled. "No problem. Is there anything else you'd like?" Alicia could see the manager was expecting a sale.

Gilly eyed the chocolates behind the counter. Then she walked over to the Valentine's display and removed a heart-shaped box that Alicia recognized was the same as the one from which Sheila had eaten the poisonous chocolate. "How much is this?"

"It's on sale for five dollars, but I'll give it to you for three."

Gilly reached into her purse and took out a five. She placed it on the counter. "No. I'll pay the five. You were nice enough to show me your class list."

Margaret rang up the sale. "Anything for you?" she asked Alicia.

Alicia realized she hadn't said a word since coming into the store. She was about to decline when she eyed a dark chocolate assortment by the counter. It wasn't on sale and she was trying to watch her calories, but she felt bad about not making a purchase. Besides, dark chocolates were her favorites. "How much is that box?" she asked pointing to the Cocoa Cocoa Dark Chocolate Assortment.

"That's one of our bestsellers. It's twenty dollars. I'm sorry I can't mark it down for you."

"It's okay," Alicia said, taking a twenty from her purse. Even though John might think it frivolous of her to spend so much money on chocolate, he'd enjoy sharing a few pieces with her. Margaret thanked her and wished her and Gilly a good day. Before they left the store, Gilly asked, "When is your assistant here?"

"Clara will be in tonight, and she also works tomorrow one to four and Wednesday and Thursday nights five to nine."

Gilly thanked her again, and she and Alicia walked out of the store toting brown Cocoa Cocoa shopping bags.

Gilly didn't say another word until they were seated in Alicia's car. "I think whoever took that class was using an alias. I didn't ask for their descriptions because Margaret probably wouldn't remember them, but I think we should go back tonight to speak with the assistant."

"You can go back if you want, Gilly, but I don't feel comfortable about lying to my husband, and it's not a good idea for you to keep this from Ramsay either."

"He'll thank me if I can get a good lead for him. Now where do you want to go for lunch?"

***

They ended up dining at La Bella. John had promised Alicia they'd take a rain date on their Valentine's dinner that was postponed after the incident at the library. However, Gilly insisted that their pizza was the best, and the place had a different mood at lunchtime than it did at dinner. People dressed more casually, and the candles that usually lit the tables were replaced with fresh flowers during the day. The lunch prices were also considerably lower than the dinner costs.

Lucia, the daughter of the restaurant's owners, greeted them as they entered. "Good afternoon, Alicia, Gilly. Long time, no see. What have you ladies been up to? How are the twins? They must be so big now."

Alicia realized she hadn't eaten in Cobble Corner's fine dining restaurant in over a year. "Yes, they're getting into everything now. We haven't had much time to eat out, but John and I are planning to come here for dinner again soon."

Lucia smiled. "You should make it a date night. Here, I have some seats by the window." She led them to a table that overlooked the outside of Cobble Corner. The trees were still bare with a light dusting of snow covering their branches. At night, when the lights were turned on outside, they would be a romantic sight.

Lucia handed them a menu. "We have a few luncheon specials on the center page. I'll be right back to take your orders."

"I already know what I'm having," Gilly said after Lucia stepped away. "Want to split a pie?"

"That's eight pieces, Gilly. I'm watching my weight."

"I can always bring some leftovers to the inn. My kids are crazy about pizza."

"Okay then, but I only want one slice."

"Alicia, you look great. I'm the one who should worry. I need to keep my body in shape for Ron. We're newlyweds, after all."

Alicia laughed. "Ramsay has his own weight battles." She changed the subject. "I wonder if Lucia's read the paper and seen the story about Sheila and Kevin?"

"I was going to ask her. Waitresses make great witnesses to small town crimes."

Alicia was sorry she'd opened her mouth. "Gilly, you can't go around interrogating everyone. It'll get back to Ramsay."

"I don't care if it does, and I'm not interrogating. I'm chatting." She placed her menu face down and pushed it to the side. Making eye contact with Lucia who was serving another customer across from them, she gave a light wave of her hand to signal her over.

"Ready to order?"

"Yes, ma'am. We'll split the La Bella Pie, extra cheese, please."

"Is that all? A salad? Drink?"

Gilly looked at Alicia. "I'll just have water."

"Me, too," Alicia said.

As Lucia turned to go, Gilly called her back. "Lucia, have you read the paper today?"

The waitress paused. "There's a copy in the back, but I haven't had a chance to read it. The breakfast crowd was large for a Saturday. Was any important news in it?"

Alicia winced. In the past, the most interesting events the paper reported included people falling from the church steps or a bicycle being stolen by a sibling. That changed when three crimes occurred in town the December before last.

"Sheila Whitehead was poisoned at the library staff party," Alicia announced, her voice calm to be talking about attempted murder.

"Oh, my God! Is she okay?" Lucia nearly dropped her notepad.

"She's in the hospital but should be home today."

"What happened? Do they know who did it? Who would possibly want to hurt Sheila? She's so sweet." Lucia's dark eyes implored them for answers.

"Someone left a box of chocolates for her at the reference desk. She ate one and was poisoned," Gilly explained. "My husband is investigating, but his prime suspect, who was seen on the library's surveillance tape, was recently found murdered in his car."

"What?" Lucia's mouth opened. "That sounds terrible. Who was killed?"

"Kevin Tucker."

Lucia gasped. "Oh, no. That young man who was friends with Andy. He was doing courier work, wasn't he? He delivered some food for us once to a sick family. I know he had a bad background, but he seemed to have straightened himself out. What a shame. Andy must be devastated."

"We haven't talked to him yet, but I'm sure he is," Gilly said.

Alicia didn't like the way her friend said that. Surely, she wasn't going to suggest they speak with Andy next.

Gilly insisted on paying the bill. "I was the one who asked you to lunch, and it's the least I can do since you're assisting me in this investigation."

"Is that a bribe?"

Gilly smiled. "I'd like to think of it as a token of my friendship."

"And what do I owe you for that token?"

Gilly placed a few singles as Lucia's tip under her empty glass. "Lunch was pretty quick. I think we'll have time to visit Andy before you have to meet John to bring the kids to Mac's house."

Alicia knew it. She could hardly contain her anger. "No, Gilly. Andy's grieving for his friend right now. I'm sure your husband's spoken to him already."

"I didn't say anything about questioning, Andy. I'd like to pay my respects to him."

Alicia wasn't convinced her friend was being honest. "You can pay your respects at the wake."

Before Gilly could protest further, Lucia came back to the table, took the envelope with Gilly's check, and pocketed the cash under the glass. "Thank you, ladies. Have a great day." As they walked out, the waitress added, "Alicia, don't forget to bring your cute kids in with John soon and if you see Sheila, please tell her I hope she feels better."

***

To get back to the parking lot, they had to walk past the *Cobble Cove Courier* office. There was a closed sign in the window and a stack of newspapers by the door. Gilly stopped and went over to the bundle where she removed the top two papers.

"What are you doing, Gilly?"

"I haven't read the story. Have you?"

Alicia hadn't. After John electronically submitted his story to the intern whom Andy had hired when he'd become Editor-in-Chief of the paper, it had been printed in the early morning hours and distributed to the businesses in Cobble Corner. Chances were the homes that subscribed hadn't yet gotten their issues.

Alicia took the paper Gilly handed her. The front page headline read, "Library Director Poisoned, Courier Murdered." Two photos were featured next to one another, Sheila and Kevin. Alicia skimmed the rest of the article. "We have to keep this away from Sheila."

"She'll read it eventually, Ali. We get copies at the library."

Alicia put her paper back on the stack. "The latter, the better. She's just getting out of the hospital today. Let's get going. John must be home from the children's museum already."

Gilly put her paper under her arm and walked with Alicia to her car. When they were seated inside, she said, "Can you do me a favor and drop me by Andy's house on your way home?"

"Gilly, I thought we'd decided you weren't going there?"

"No. We decided you're not coming with me."

Alicia sighed and started the car. "I'll go, but only for a few minutes. I want to make sure you don't upset Andy more than he already is."

As Alicia pulled out of the spot, a dark blue Chevy claimed it. Alicia recognized it as Professor Anderson's rental. Gilly noticed, too. "Wait," she said. "That's Ryan's car. Drive around the lot slowly and see where he's headed."

"I'm not going to tail him."

"I'm not asking you to tail him. We just need to see where he's headed."

Alicia didn't want to argue with Gilly, so she made a slow circle around Cobble Corner. As they rounded the parking lot on their final loop, Gilly pointed out the window exclaiming, "There he is. He's going into Cocoa Cocoa."

Chapter Seventeen

"Calm down, Gilly. Maybe he's picking up a get-well gift for Sheila."

"That doesn't make sense, Alicia. All they sell in there is chocolate, and I'm sure that's the last thing Sheila would want right now."

"What are you suggesting? You really think he would go back there if that's where he made the poisoned candy?"

"Ron taught me that criminals always return to the scene of the crime. Maybe he's in cahoots with Margaret Simmons."

"Now you're reaching." Alicia stepped on the gas. "We're getting out of here. If you want to share this with Ramsay, that's fine with me, but you better not let him know we were snooping into his case."

"What I tell my husband is my prerogative. Do you remember where Andy lives?"

Alicia took a deep breath and let it out. "Yes, Gilly. John took me there once. It's near the church." She drove a few blocks and turned on to Quarry Avenue. Many of the streets in Cobble Cove had names related to stones and rocks. Her own street was called Stone's Throw Road.

Alicia pulled over to the curb in front of the white ranch located mid-block. The blinds at the windows were drawn, and she almost feared no one was home, but Andy's car was in the driveway.

"I don't have a good feeling about this, Gilly," Alicia said as they walked to the door. Gilly ignored her and tapped the bell.

A few minutes later, Mrs. Phillips answered. Her auburn hair, tipped with gray, was loose around her heart shaped face as if she hadn't bothered to brush it. Dark bags sat heavily under her blue eyes. Despite her tired and sad appearance, she managed a smile. "Alicia. Gilly. I guess you're here to see Andy. Thank you for coming."

Alicia felt even worse about disturbing their mourning, but Gilly said, "How is Andy? Is he up to speaking with us?"

"He's in his room, but I'm sure he'll be happy to see you. Please come in."

Alicia followed Gilly into the Phillips' pleasant home. Andy's mother invited them to sit on the sofa above which hung photos of Andy, his younger brother Alan, and their parents, taken when Mr. Phillips was alive.

"Would either of you like something to drink while you wait for Andy?"

They shook their heads. "We just had lunch," Gilly said.

"Okay then. I'll go upstairs and tell him you're here." When she walked away, Gilly said, "I guess Alan is out."

"I think he works Saturdays. He shares the car with his mother. Andy told John he's saving money for a used one. Things have been tough since their father passed away. I'm sure this was another blow to them. Andy had Kevin over here a few times for dinner."

A few minutes later, Andy came down the stairs followed by his mother. His shoulders were slumped, making his tall, thin frame seem smaller. His mop of red hair also looked unbrushed, and the blue eyes, like his mom's, were watery and red-rimmed.

"Hi," he said in a slightly choked voice. Mrs. Phillips slipped away to give them room to talk.

"Hello, Andy," Alicia said. "So sorry for your loss." She always found it hard to say the right words of sympathy and recalled some of the false sounding comments people at her first husband's wake had issued.

Gilly said, "We wanted to see how you were holding up."

Andy shrugged, remained standing. "Not too well, but it's nice of you to come. Your husband was here last night. He asked me a few questions about Kevin." He said the name on a choke.

"Why don't you sit down," Gilly said.

Andy plopped himself in the chair next to the couch. He rubbed a hand through his hair. "I don't understand. Kevin was doing so well. He was planning to go back to school when he saved some money from the courier job. He was only twenty-three, a year older than me."

Alicia's heart ached for Andy's sorrow. She knew how unfair life could be.

Gilly asked, "Did Kevin keep a record of his courier jobs?"

"Yes, I told the sheriff that. Unfortunately, he recorded them in a notebook. I kept bugging him to put the information on computer. What's worse is that he didn't record his cash sales. I don't blame him because he kept that money to himself, but the Sheriff said it'll be hard to track down the person who hired him to deliver those chocolates if they paid him that way."

Alicia was hoping Gilly would be satisfied with that reply, but she should've known how persistent her friend could be. "Did you speak with him this week? Did he mention any of his Valentine's Day jobs?"

Andy shook his head. "Your husband asked me that, too. I spoke with Kev on Wednesday. We were planning to catch a movie this weekend. Wait . . ." He turned toward Gilly. "I do remember something. He told me had a lot of deliveries for Valentine's Day. The flower shop in town had hired him to do some deliveries because they were overwhelmed with orders. But he also said someone had contacted him from the ad he'd placed in the *Courier*. I'd let him run it for free. Oh, gosh." His voice choked again. "Maybe I shouldn't have done that."

"Andy, you couldn't have known the person who was planning to have Kevin deliver those chocolates to the library would answer that ad. You can't blame yourself." Alicia understood how powerful an emotion guilt could be. She'd experienced it herself, and John had been so wrapped up on it after his wife died in childbirth that it almost stopped him from forming a relationship with her.

"Who did he say called him?" Gilly asked, trying to bring Andy back to her original question. Alicia felt that she was being inconsiderate, but she also understood the importance of following through on this lead. It seemed this information had not been given to Ramsay.

"He didn't say, Mrs. Ramsay. He just thought it odd that the caller didn't want to do business at their home. Usually, when people have packages to deliver, they asked him to pick them up at their house."

"Did the caller go to his house?" Alicia could see the wheels turning in Gilly's head.

"No. They asked to meet him near the park on Thursday night. That's what was strange."

Alicia found it hard to believe that Andy wouldn't remember this when he'd been questioned by Ramsay, and Gilly must've thought so, too, because she added, "Why didn't you think of this when my husband spoke with you? It sounds like an important lead."

Andy lowered his eyes. "Sorry, but I was so upset. It was right after I'd learned Kevin was dead. I wasn't thinking straight. I'll be willing to talk to the sheriff again if you let him know, but there's not much else to say. I don't even know if the person who met Kev by the park was a man or a woman. All he said was, 'Someone called me and wants me to pick up a delivery by the park. They're offering me some big bucks, so who am I to question it?'"

"Big bucks? Did he say how much?"

"No, ma'am." He looked back up at Gilly.

Alicia said, "Thanks, Andy. I know this is tough for you but try not to blame yourself."

She was relieved when Gilly stood up and said, "You've given us some important information. I'll be sure to share it with Ron. We have some other things to do today, but we wanted to stop by to give our regards to you on the loss of your friend."

Alicia hoped that statement was partially true. She joined Gilly as Andy walked them to the door.

"I'm sorry I can't help further with your husband's investigation," he said, "but my mom has arranged a service with Pastor Ellen, the new pastor at Cobble Cove Community Church. It's tomorrow night at seven. I hope you both can attend and John, too."

"We'll be there," Alicia said. Gilly nodded.

***

As they drove back to the inn, Gilly said, "What did you make of what Andy said? Didn't I tell you it's worth following up on Ron's questioning?"

"Yes, but we didn't learn too much more. Were you telling the truth when you said you'd share what Andy said with Ramsay? How are you going to explain how you got the information?"

"That's easy. I'll be honest with my husband and tell him I paid my respects to Andy and that he'd remembered something he forget to mention about a recent job of Kevin's."

"That sounds okay, I guess. Are you saying anything about going to Cocoa Cocoa?"

"I don't think that's necessary. However, I'm planning to go back tonight to speak with the assistant who gave that chocolate class. Even though none of our suspects are on the list, I think they may have used an alias in which case the assistant, Clara Wiggs, might be able to describe those who attended and give us a clue."

"Us? Gilly, I can't go back with you. What would I tell John? I've already wasted part of the day away from my family."

"He'll understand. Say we're doing some shopping. It isn't exactly a lie. We'll be at Cobble Corner. It won't take long."

"I'll think about it." Alicia pulled up at the inn. Before Gilly got out, she said, "We learned a lot today. Don't forget, we saw Lover Boy Anderson go into the chocolate shop. That alone is worth investigating. In addition, we found out that Kevin was offered a lot of money to deliver those chocolates. I'm sure the Professor has that kind of cash."

"You have a point, Gilly, but I'm not rushing to conclusions yet. My concern is Sheila. When I get home, John and I are going to visit her."

"Give her my regards. Maybe I'll visit her tomorrow." She opened the car door and got out. Walking over to the driver's side, she said. "Thanks for coming with me, Alicia. I know you aren't too thrilled about our investigating together again, but I think we make a good team."

Before she could reply, Gilly walked to the inn's door. Alicia watched as it opened, and Mrs. Burke let her in. *How long is that woman staying in Cobble Cove?* She thought. As much as one might like a small town, there was a limit to how much one could see there. Would she be as enchanted with the place once she learned that an attempted murder had occurred in the library and the suspect had been shot dead?

Chapter Eighteen

When she pulled into her driveway, Alicia saw that John and the kids were home. He stood at the door, and she assumed he'd been waiting for her. But as she came up the walk, she saw his face was creased with concern.

"John, what's wrong?"

"Johnny got sick at the museum. He's running a fever. He seemed fine when we left, but he threw up right on the brontosaur statue's foot. Carol was so upset."

"Why didn't you call me?" Alicia rushed into the house.

"I didn't want to disturb your lunch with Gilly. I'm sure it's just a stomach bug. His temperature is only a bit over 100. That's not so high for a kid."

"I guess that rules out going to see Sheila."

"No. One of us should go. I can stay here and watch him. Why don't you go?"

Alicia hesitated. She hated the fact that John was able to spend more time with the twins than she did because of her full-time job. "I'm his mother. I should take care of him while he's sick."

"Come upstairs with me. You'll see he's okay. You can leave him for a few minutes."

They walked upstairs together. As soon as she entered the nursery, Carol ran to Alicia. "Mommy, Johnny pooked in the mooseum. We go back?"

"Not today, honey, and don't get too close to your brother. You don't want to catch his bug."

"Bug?" Her eyes darted around wildly.

Alicia laughed. "I mean you don't want to come down with his sickness." She approached Johnny's bed. The boy lay there, his dark hair flattened off his face, his cheeks red.

"Hey, honey. How do you feel?"

He squinted his eyes and rubbed his stomach. "Tummy hurts."

She placed a hand on his head. "You're still warm. Do you still feel like you're going to throw up?"

"Dunno."

She turned to her husband. "John, get a rag and rinse it in cool water for his head and also a pan in case he's sick again."

John did as she said and returned with both items. He handed her the cloth that she lay across Johnny's forehead. She placed the bowl on the floor next to the bed. "If you feel very sick again, you can use that," she said. "This way, you don't have to worry about making it to the bathroom."

Johnny nodded.

"Me Johnny nuss?" Carol asked. She seemed more enthused with that idea than going back to the museum.

"Sure, sweetie. Keep an eye on him but let him rest."

"Take temp-ture?"

John said, "I can show you how to do that while Mommy goes to visit her boss who just came home from the hospital."

"John, I should stay."

"Ali, I'm totally capable of watching these two a few more minutes, and now I have an assistant." He patted his daughter's head.

Alicia sighed. "Okay. I'll go, but I'll be back soon." She bent down and gave Johnny a kiss on his warm cheek. "You feel better. You have Nurse Carol watching you and your dad. I won't be long."

As she made her exit, she caught John at the door. In a whisper, she said, "If he takes a turn for the worse, call me on my cell immediately. I'll be as quick as I can."

"Don't worry. Everything will be fine. Give my regards to Sheila."

As Alicia drove toward Sheila's house, she suddenly realized she should've picked up a get-well gift. She hated to delay her trip, but the town's flower shop was on her way. Located in a cluster of stores on Main Street that didn't get as much business as the Cobble Corner shops, Cobble Florist still had a display of Valentine's roses in its windows. She expected they were on sale after the holiday.

As she entered the store, she was assaulted by the scents of flowers and fresh greenery. Daisy Parker, the sixty-something year old owner who folks liked to tease about her name, greeted her with a smile. "Alicia, I haven't seen you in a while. I thought for sure John would've come by last week to pick up some roses for you."

"I told him not to get me any this year, Daisy. He gave me jewelry instead." She fingered the cameo at her throat.

"How lovely, but maybe he'll surprise you with a bunch for your birthday."

"That's not until October." Since Alicia had turned forty, she didn't care to celebrate another year. "The reason I'm dropping by is because I need a get-well arrangement."

"Ah. For Sheila, I imagine?"

So word had already spread. "Yes, she's home from the hospital, and I'm going to visit her. What do you have?"

Daisy walked toward the back of the store where several beribboned boxes, vases, and other unique settings were displayed. Some featured balloons. Others included teas and chocolates. All held a beautiful variety of blooms.

"These are nice for get wells." Daisy indicated a few choices to the left of the counter.

"Sheila likes tea," Alicia said. "The one with the carnations and lilies in the bright yellow teapot would be nice." Yellow was Sheila's favorite color, and the arrangement even included a few chamomile tea bags and a lemon-colored balloon with 'Get Well' written on it. The tag indicated it was only $20 which was a bargain considering the cost of the teapot alone.

"Good choice," Daisy said. As she carefully brought the arrangement to the counter for Alicia to pay, the shop door opened. Alicia glanced back to see who'd entered. She drew in a breath when she recognized the man walking toward them. It was Ryan Anderson.

Daisy recognized him, too. "Professor Anderson. Back for more flowers for your special lady? So sorry to hear what happened to her."

Ryan's expression was somber. "Sheila's coming home today. I brought the Valentine roses to the hospital, but I'd like to get something cheerier for her." He glanced around. "Those yellow mums might do the trick."

He already knew Sheila's favorite color, Alicia thought.

"Do you want those in a vase?"

"Just wrap them, please."

"Right after I take care of Alicia."

The professor suddenly turned his eyes on her. "Oh, hello, there, Mrs. McKinney. Sorry to be rude. I'm eager to visit Sheila. I wanted to bring her home, but Sheriff Ramsay insisted on that. I can understand after what happened to her that he would want to make sure things are safe in her house."

"I happen to be going there, too. I'm bringing that arrangement in the teapot."

"Very nice. I'm sure Sheila will enjoy that."

Daisy rang up Alicia's sale. She then rolled out what Alicia assumed was leftover white tissue paper decorated with hearts for Valentine's Day, cut, wrapped, and taped it around a bunch of the yellow Chrysanthemums Ryan had requested. She handed him a small packet.

"Remember to cut the stems under warm water and add this. It'll make them last longer."

"Thank you," he said as he paid her. He turned to Alicia. "I guess I'll see you at Sheila's place."

"Yes, I'm going there now."

He walked her to her car which was parked right behind his in front of the flower shop. "Alicia, if I may, I want to thank you for your kind concern for Sheila. She's quite fond of you."

Alicia wasn't sure how to respond to that, but she realized she had an opportunity to ask him why he'd been at the chocolate shop earlier. "The feeling is mutual, Professor Anderson." She refrained from using his first name. "But may I ask you a question?"

"Of course." Was she imagining that his eyes clouded?

"I dropped by Cocoa Cocoa with my friend today, and we saw you going in there afterwards. Did you happen to purchase some chocolate for Sheila, too?"

"Oh, no." His face looked genuinely disturbed. "I wouldn't do that after what happened to her. I was inquiring of the owner about who shopped there recently. It seems they had a chocolate making class the night before Sheila was poisoned. Detective Ramsay had questioned Ms. Simmons, too, but I thought maybe she'd remember something else . . ." He waved his arm without finishing the sentence.

Alicia didn't know if she believed him, but it was possible he'd been doing some of the same unofficial investigating as she and Gilly. She walked to her car and secured the flowers on the passenger side floor. Anderson got in his own car and drove off in the direction of Sheila's house. Alicia followed.

***

Alicia and Ryan pulled up at the yellow stucco ranch at the same time, but Alicia got out of her car first. Ryan, holding the wrapped mums, came up behind her. An old feeling of apprehension gripped Alicia. She'd been stalked once and still felt uncomfortable when people followed her. After she rang the bell, they stood on the stoop waiting for Sheila to answer. Alicia noticed an unmarked car parked a few yards away with Ramsay at the wheel munching something that may have been a donut.

When Sheila opened the door, Alicia expected her to be in a nightgown, looking pale and tired. Instead, Sheila swung the door back, fully clothed in a sweater and jeans and even wearing boots. She ignored her guests and stormed from the house. Rushing to Ramsay's car, she yelled, "Get off my property! I don't need anyone watching out for me. You're invading my privacy."

Alicia felt her mouth drop. Ryan shrugged. Ramsay looked like he was choking. He got out of his car and, composing himself, faced Sheila. "Mrs. Whitehead, you may be in danger. We're only doing this for your own good."

She waved a finger at him. "I'm perfectly fine. I'm keeping my doors and windows locked, and I have an alarm system activated. I don't need you or your men keeping tabs on me. If you want to do something productive, spend the time and resources on finding who poisoned me."

Ramsay looked rebuffed. "Very well. If that's what you want. I'll do just that." He got back behind his wheel and sped off in a cloud of dust.

Sheila walked back toward them. "Sorry about that." Her face changed when she saw Ryan. "Are those for me? How thoughtful of you. I left my hospital flowers with the staff, so they could give them to others who needed them."

Alicia felt disappointed that Sheila was ignoring her gift. "These are for you, too," she said.

"Oh, Alicia. Yes, those are beautiful also. Please come in."

They entered the house. Sheila asked them to place the flowers on her kitchen table, and she would find a spot for them. Ryan said, "Do you have a vase? I'll put these in water and add the growth packet the florist gave me."

"I can take care of that."

"No," he insisted. "You should be resting. Sit down with Alicia, and I'll do it."

Sheila tossed back her red hair which was restrained with a paisley headband. "Thank you. There are vases in the top cabinet." She glanced at Alicia. "Men? They like to baby us." Alicia thought her giggle was like a teenager's. This was a different woman than the one who'd just told off the town sheriff. "Let's go into the living room, shall we?"

***

"Have a seat, Alicia. Would you like some coffee or tea? That teapot full of flowers was a wonderful idea."

So Sheila had noticed. "No, thank you. I don't want anything. John's home with Johnny. He got sick with a stomach bug in the children's museum this morning."

"That's too bad. I know how nasty those can be. Julie was prone to them."

At the mention of Sheila's daughter's name, Alicia felt a bit guilty. She avoided Sheila's gaze as she took a seat next to her on the beige couch.

"Speaking of Julie, she called me when I'd just gotten home from the hospital. She wants to visit. I didn't say a word to her about what happened to me, of course, but I think someone may have contacted her. It doesn't matter. I'd love to see her."

Alicia kept her eyes focused on the photos that lined the living room walls. The largest one featured Sheila sitting next to her husband Tom and holding a baby Julie. It must've been taken shortly before he died suddenly of a brain aneurysm.

"When is she coming?"

Sheila smiled. "I thought she'd wait until the winter recess during President's week when her kids are off from school, but she's coming by herself on Monday. I don't know how she managed to get off from work so quickly, and I assume her husband is taking some time off to watch the kids. She's only stopping by for a day or two. I can't imagine flying all the way here just to do that, but she worked in the airlines once before she got her job at the travel agency. That's how she met Ben."

Alicia realized she didn't know much about Sheila's family except that they lived in California. "I look forward to meeting her," she said as she took another glance at the other photos on the wall. One of them was a photo taken of Sheila's wedding. Sheila looked so young standing in her white gown next to her handsome tuxedoed husband. On one side of the group gathered in a beautiful garden setting were the members of the wedding party, the maid-of-honor and the bridesmaids in lovely golden gowns and the Best Man and groomsmen in matching black tuxedos. The parents of the couple were also in the picture. The shot must've been taken more than thirty-five years ago, and the only person Alicia had ever met was Sheila. Yet, someone else looked familiar to her. She was about to comment when Ryan called out from the kitchen, "Hate to bother you, Sheila, but where do you keep your vases? I'm having trouble finding them."

Sheila smiled. "Excuse me, Alicia. Let me go help him."

Alicia got up to take a closer look at the photo but then she heard a clatter in the kitchen as if something had fallen. She rushed to the door and saw Sheila standing amid shards of broken glass. Ryan faced her by the sink with a knife in his hand.

Chapter Nineteen

Alicia gasped. Her hand went instinctively to her cell phone. She prayed Ramsay hadn't gone far since Sheila sent him away. But Sheila was laughing. Why was she laughing?

"I'm so clumsy," she said. "I went to get a vase and dropped it."

Alicia now saw that the knife Ryan was holding was covered in greenery. He turned and placed it in the sink. "I'll wash that later. Let me give you a hand cleaning that up." He grabbed a dustpan and broom from next to the trash bin and started sweeping.

Alicia's heartbeat returned to normal. Ryan had simply used one of the knives in Sheila's knife block to chop the stems of the flowers he'd brought her. Entering the kitchen, she saw the chrysanthemums on the counter next to the sink. "Can I help?" she offered.

Sheila said, "I think it's best if Ryan gets another vase from that top cabinet. He can reach it better than us." Even though Sheila was taller than Alicia, Ryan was more than a head taller than the two of them.

Ryan finished sweeping up the glass and emptied the pan into the trash bin. "Why you keep vases up so high, I can't imagine, Sheila."

"I don't have much use for them," she explained. "I like to keep my more important kitchen items closer."

Ryan reached up and brought down a crystal vase. "You might be using these a lot more if I have any say in bringing you flowers. Will this one do for the mums?"

Alicia saw Sheila's face change. "Uh, yes. It will. Thank you." But it seemed she was reluctant to let Ryan use the one he'd chosen. Alicia wondered why.

***

After the flowers had been placed, Ryan's next to Alicia's in the open cabinet Sheila used for displaying curios and knickknacks as well as another photo of her and Tom, they sat in the living room. Sheila and Ryan took the couch this time, and Alicia moved to a chair. She wondered how Ryan felt about seeing all these mementos of Sheila's late husband.

"I can't stay that much longer," Alicia said. "I'm worried about Johnny, but I'm glad you're looking well, Sheila."

Ryan said, "You go ahead, Alicia. I'll keep Sheila company."

Although she knew Ryan hadn't been threatening Sheila with the knife, Alicia was still reluctant to leave him alone with her. The scene in the kitchen brought back some of her earlier suspicions.

"Maybe Sheila needs some rest. She just got home from the hospital." She was hoping her words would persuade him to leave with her, but that wasn't the case.

"I'm not tired at all," Sheila said.

Ryan added, "Now that you kicked your bodyguard away, I'd be happy to take the sheriff's place protecting you."

Sheila giggled again, and Alicia felt that sinking feeling in her stomach. She was relieved when the doorbell suddenly rang. Sheila got up to answer it and, a few seconds later, led Donald into the room. He was holding an envelope in his hand.

"Looks like the whole reference staff is here," Ryan said, smiling.

"Hello Professor Anderson, Alicia. I heard Sheila was home and wanted to see how she was doing. This is from Roger and me." He handed Sheila the envelope.

"Thank you, Donald. Please have a seat. Now I really must make some coffee or tea. Are you staying, Alicia?"

"A few more minutes, but please don't go to any trouble."

"No trouble at all," Sheila said. "I'd like something myself." As she headed for the kitchen, Ryan got up. "Be right back, folks. I'll give her a hand."

When they were gone, Alicia whispered to Donald, "I need to leave soon, but I didn't want to go while he was still here. Can you stay and keep an eye on him?"

Donald seemed surprised. He answered in the same low tone, "You still suspect him? My money's on horse lady. I can stay a bit, but I can't promise to wait for him. He'll probably hang around trying to get in her pants."

"Donald!" Alicia exclaimed, raising her voice so that Sheila, reentering the room with a teapot on a tray and some mugs, said, "What's going on out here? Are you two arguing over something?"

"Donald just told me one of his off-color jokes," Alicia replied.

"Is that so? Let's hear it, buddy?" Ryan said joining them with another tray that held some cookies and a small coffeepot. He pulled out two fold-up tables. Kicking out the legs, he opened them and placed his tray on it and moved the other to Sheila, so she could put down hers.

"I don't think so," Donald said.

"Oh, c'mon, I'm sure Sheila could use a funny story to cheer her up."

"I'm not sad, Ryan. Let's have our tea and coffee and some nice conversation."

Alicia took this as a chance to make her leave. "Sorry I can't stay for that, but I have to go and check my son." She walked to Sheila and gave her a light kiss on the cheek. "Feel better. If you need anything, please call us."

"Thank you, Alicia. Take a few cookies for the kids. I'm sure that'll make them feel good."

She handed her a napkin and wrapped a few of the cookies in it.

As Alicia left, Donald waved to her and winked. She had a feeling that, despite his reluctance to promise, he'd stay until Ryan left.

**

The door was open when Alicia got home. She rushed inside, fear building inside her that Johnny was worse. But when she entered, she heard Carol's high-squealed laughter and Johnny's quieter giggles. She found the kids seated on either side of their father upstairs in the bay window of the nursery as he read to them one of their favorite books, *The Three Little Pigs.* "And he huffed, and he puffed, and he blew the house down," said John as both kids puffed up their cheeks and blew breaths out mimicking the wolf.

As she tiptoed into the room, the reading stopped. "Hey, there, Mommy. Just in time for bedtime stories." Alicia went over and put her hand on Johnny's head. It felt cooler. "No temp-a-chur," he said.

"Mommy's glad. How's the tummy?"

"All better." He smiled, showing three missing baby teeth.

"Join us?" John offered.

Alicia sat in the rocker next to the window. "Do I have a part?"

John's grin matched his son's. "You can be the pig in the straw house."

"I'm honored."

After the kids were left to sleep, Alicia and John slipped from the room.

"How is Sheila?" he asked.

"Her normally feisty self. She kicked Ramsay off patrol and threatened him if she found any of his men near her house."

John laughed. "Sounds like she's recovered."

"Ryan was there and then Donald came. I rushed back for Johnny. I was worried." She didn't tell him she still suspected Ryan and was hesitant to leave him alone with Sheila.

"You shouldn't have hurried back. They were in capable hands."

"I know that, but still. . ."

"What's on the agenda for tonight?" His blue eyes lit up, and she knew what he was thinking.

"I might do some writing on our book. I haven't had a chance to review that last chapter you added."

"And after that . . ?"

"I don't know, John. I'm a bit tired. Rain check?"

"Sure. I think I'll work on my laptop in bed. You can have the office to yourself."

"Thanks." John knew that Alicia needed total quiet and concentration while she wrote. He, on the other hand, liked to listen to a playlist of tunes for inspiration. When they worked together, he used earplugs, but she still found it a distraction.

"Thank you." She went downstairs and turned on the computer. As it booted up, the phone rang. Answering, she heard Gilly's breathless voice on the other end. "Alicia. You're never going to believe this."

Used to her friend's dramatics, she replied, "Try me. Oh, and by the way, I was at Sheila's house today with our friend, the Professor. Donald showed up, and I hope he stayed to keep an eye on him because Sheila sent your husband away with a threat if she saw him or any of his officers near her house."

"I know all about that, Alicia, but Sheila has nothing to fear from Ryan. I found out who made those chocolates Thursday night."

"What?" Now Alicia was genuinely surprised. "We saw the list. There was no one on it that we knew."

Gilly paused for suspense. "That's because we didn't consider that one of the persons signing up would cancel and someone else would get their spot."

"Where did you get this information? Did Margaret's assistant tell you?"

"Yep. I said I was considering taking the class and wanted to speak to someone who already took it for a recommendation. When she gave me the name of the person who enjoyed the last class the most, I was shocked."

"Gilly, get to the point." Alicia was losing her patience.

"One of the women had dropped out and the person who replaced her was . . ." She paused again. "Mrs. Horse Lady herself, Rhonda Kleisman."

Chapter Twenty

Alicia recalled Mrs. Kleisman bringing the chocolate cake as a peace offering to Sheila and Donald's words when she told him to watch Ryan, "My money's on Horse Lady."

"Did you tell Ramsay?"

"Sure did, and I think he was proud of me. He's going to get a search warrant for Kleisman's house. It might take some time because it's the weekend, but he's hoping to put a push on it and get it by tomorrow."

"What does he hope to find there?"

"Any traces of the poison that was used in the chocolates. They think the substance was injected into the pieces. Kleisman must've brought the box home and used a dropper or a syringe to put it in."

"Do they know what type of poison was used?"

"Ron wouldn't say, but he mentioned that not all the pieces were tampered with, only the dark chocolate ones."

"Strange. I guess Mrs. Kleisman figured out Sheila likes dark chocolate more than milk. I guess we just wait until Ramsay checks her house."

"Not exactly." Alicia didn't like the way Gilly's voice took on a higher-pitched tone.

"What do you mean? Gilly, you aren't thinking . . ."

"Yep. We pay a visit to Mrs. Horse Lady."

"At this hour? John just put the kids to sleep. I was about to work on our book."

"Ron is at the station working late, and my kids are at sleepovers tonight, so this is a perfect time. I'll lock up the place and pick you up in ten minutes."

Alicia checked the clock on her computer. It was 9:30. "I don't know why I let you talk me into these things. This could be dangerous. What should I tell John?"

"Just say you're going out with me. Can't a girl have a girl's night out?"

"Gilly, whoever killed Kevin used a gun. If it's Kleisman, she most likely still has it and could turn it on us."

"She won't expect us, and I'm bringing my pepper spray."

Alicia sighed. "Okay. I'm only going because I know you'll go by yourself if I don't."

"That's my pal. See you in a few."

***

Alicia was thankful that John didn't question her when she told him she was going out with Gilly. He looked up from his computer, nodded, and said, "Have a good time."

"I won't be long. Gilly wanted to show me a new blouse at Chloe's closet. They're staying open late tonight for a special sale." She hated to lie using a story she concocted, but John seemed to accept it.

Gilly arrived at the house in precisely the ten minutes she'd promised. She was wearing a trench coat, and Alicia imagined she was playing the part of a detective. She hoped their late visit to Kleisman wouldn't be a fatal one. Pepper spray was no match for a gun.

***

What Alicia and Gilly hadn't imagined when they'd knocked on Kleisman's door was that one of her kids would open it. Alicia knew Kleisman was divorced and had three kids ranging in age from eight to fifteen, and there was no mistaking that the older girl was the one who answered. Her face was as dour as her mother's, and she was well on her way to the same weight problem.

"Who are you?" she asked in a voice that was a younger version of her mom's.

"We're friends of your mother's from the library," Gilly said. Alicia didn't consider herself Rhonda Kleisman's friend and she knew Gilly didn't either, but the cover was believable.

"My mother doesn't have any friends at the library, but I'll tell her you're here."

As the girl scooted back inside yelling, "Mother, some strange ladies from the library are here to see you," Alicia heard the background noise of a television playing.

She and Gilly stepped into what could only be described as a mess. Clothes were tossed all over, open bags of snacks lay spilling their contents on a carpet that looked like it hadn't been vacuumed in years, and books were strewn everywhere, some with torn pages or smashed bindings as if someone had stepped on them with boots. Alicia recognized the first two mysteries in her and John's series and stifled a cry. Kleisman sat with her slippered feet up on the couch munching a candy bar, eyes trained on the movie she was watching, oblivious to the chaos around her and of Gilly and Alicia entering. A girl ran in circles around the room, and another giggled from the top of a stairway. The daughter who let them in said, "You'll have to wait for the commercial. She doesn't like to be disturbed when she's watching her shows."

Gilly gazed around the room and then took a few steps forward. She cleared her throat. "Excuse me, Mrs. Kleisman, but we need to talk to you. Now."

Alicia was surprised at her friend's command, but it caught Kleisman's attention. She turned her head. "Mrs. Ramsay and Mrs. McKinney from the library. Have you come to collect more fines?"

"No. We don't do that. Your record is currently clear." Gilly emphasized the word "clear." It looked like several of the books on the floor, including Alicia's, were damaged beyond repair.

"So, what do you want? I'm busy." She faced the set again.

Gilly, straightening her shoulders, strode to the TV and turned it off. Alicia gasped. The running girl froze in place, as if a game of musical chairs was going on and the sound had suddenly stopped. Kleisman jumped off the couch, nearly falling over one of the books by her feet. "How dare you. If your husband wasn't the sheriff, I'd have him come and arrest you for trespassing in my home."

"Your daughter let us in, and it's rude to ignore guests."

Kleisman's face reddened. She gave her daughter, standing behind them, a glare. Then she huffed out a breath. "You have two minutes before I kick you both out."

Alicia wondered how Gilly would reply to that. She also had no idea how Ramsay and his men would be able to find anything in this house if their search warrant was approved.

Gilly looked Kleisman in the eye. Alicia admired her courage as she stood face to face with the much larger woman. "I heard that you took a chocolate making class at Cocoa Cocoa Thursday night. Is that true?"

Kleisman didn't deny the statement. "Yes. I've tried it on my own, but those baking books at the library were useless. Is that all you came here for?"

"No. Do you keep a gun in your house, Mrs. Kleisman?"

The woman seemed as shocked as Alicia at Gilly's question. "Why are you asking me these things? Did your husband put you up to this? Is he considering me a suspect in that boy's murder? I never saw that kid before. I ate the box of chocolates I made that night. I gave a few to my children. Isn't that right, Hilda?" She turned to the girl who'd opened the door. Her other kid had gone upstairs to join her giggling sister on the stairs, and they were peering down at their mother and the women from the library.

"Yes," Hilda said. "They were delicious."

Kleisman smiled. "As far as the gun, ever since I got rid of my no-good husband, I've kept one for protection. I have a license for it, and it's locked up so my kids can't get it. Ramsay can check it out. It's never been fired." She paused and took another breath. "If that's all, I'd like to get back to my movie. You can tell your husband that I won't answer any further questions without my lawyer."

"Thank you, Mrs. Kleisman," Gilly said. She turned, and, avoiding a sticky mess of crushed M&M's, walked toward the door. Alicia followed.

***

Back in Gilly's car, Alicia said, "I was surprised at you in there. I'm glad she didn't have her gun at her side when you interrupted her TV."

Gilly grinned. "What a pigsty. That woman may be a slob and a crummy mother, but I don't think she's a killer."

"Who does that leave? Are you back to suspecting Anderson?"

"Maybe we're overlooking someone, but I still haven't ruled him out. It was very odd of him to come all the way here from California to do his research."

"I spoke to Sheila's daughter who's coming here on Monday. She said she was trying to matchmake her mother with Ryan. She seems to think highly of him."

Gilly turned on her wipers. A light snow was starting to fall. "I'd like to meet that girl, but she might be as blind as Sheila to that guy's motives."

Alicia had no reply to that. She was remembering the Professor holding a knife. What would've happened if Sheila hadn't dropped the vase that alerted Alicia to come into the kitchen at that moment?

Chapter Twenty-One

Alicia felt guilty sneaking in the house after Gilly dropped her off. Tiptoeing upstairs past the nursery, she saw John was still up typing on his laptop.

"Welcome back," he said as she entered. Something in his tone was tight.

"Thanks, John. Still working?"

"Not exactly. I'm a bit stuck on this chapter. How was the sale? Didn't you get the blouse?"

Alicia had to think fast. "Uh, the store was closed by the time we got there. It's okay. It wasn't really what I wanted, anyway."

"Hmm." John closed the laptop lid. "You know you're a terrible liar, Ali."

"What do you mean?" She lowered her eyes.

"Look at me." She raised her head to see his eyes had turned to blue ice.

"I know you're sleuthing around with Gilly again, and I don't like it. You two are taking unnecessary risks. We have young children, and Gilly has her sons. I'm planning to have a talk with Ramsay and fill him in on what you two are up to. I think he'll be able to put a stop to it."

"John, please. . ."

"If you'd rather I keep this to myself, then promise me you won't lie to me again. Promise me you won't be Gilly's detecting buddy."

Alicia ran a hand through her chestnut hair, an action she did when she was nervous. "I won't lie to you again, John. I felt terrible about that, but I can't promise you that I won't help Gilly. If I turn her down, she'll just do it herself. Alone."

"Then let her." John moved his laptop to his side table. "Are you going to bed now?"

"Yes, after I use the bathroom." A few minutes later, after brushing her teeth and changing, Alicia got into bed next to John. He faced away from her. She tentatively reached out a hand. "John, I know you're upset. I don't blame you, but please understand that Gilly's my best friend. I've known her longer than you, and I know how to keep her in check. I won't let her put either of us in danger."

"Oh, no?" He turned to face her, his eyes still steely. "Have you forgotten what happened at the Holiday Inn in Clarksville last September?"

"No, I haven't, but that ended well. We caught the killer."

"Not without help. You could've both been killed."

Alicia acknowledged he was right. "I understand. Next time Gilly asks me to investigate with her, I'm refusing. I promise, John, and I mean it this time."

His eyes softened a bit. "Good." He leaned over and gave her a light kiss on the lips. "I love you, Ali. I couldn't bear it if something happened to you."

***

The sun streamed through the stained-glass windows of the church. Alicia, in her white lace wedding gown, walked down the aisle. She glanced at the man next to her. It wasn't her father who hadn't even walked her down for her first wedding because it had been an elopement, and it wasn't Mac who'd ambled next to her on his cane to give her to John. Instead, the man next to her was Ryan Anderson and the man waiting for her wasn't John but her dead husband Peter. Even though she knew this couldn't be happening, she continued her approach to the altar.

When she reached the front of the church, Ryan stepped back, so Peter could take his place. She now saw John. He was there holding the box that contained the wedding rings. He was Peter's best man. They faced the minister who Alicia was shocked to see was Sheila in a white robe. Tossing back her red hair, she read the words of the wedding ceremony and then asked if anyone saw fit that the marriage shouldn't take place. It was then that a murmur ran through those gathered. Alicia saw Rhonda Kleisman sitting in the front pew. Gilly was there, too, in her maid of honor gown with Ramsay beside her in his sheriff's uniform.

Suddenly, before Sheila could pronounce Alicia and Peter man and wife, Ryan withdrew a knife from inside his tuxedo vest and waved it at Sheila. Kleisman rushed from her seat with a box of chocolates that she scattered on the ground like wedding confetti. Alicia watched all this in a cloud of disbelief. Then a shadowy figure dressed in black wearing a black veil walked down the aisle. The person stepped up to Sheila and aimed a gun at her chest.

"No!" Alicia screamed. Other screams echoed hers as people fled from their seats. Alicia woke up, still hearing the screams.

"Ali, you okay?" It was John. "I'm going to Carol. She's crying."

Alicia tried to clear her head. "I was dreaming. What's wrong with Carol?"

"I don't know. Let's go see." John pulled on pajama bottoms.

Alicia grabbed the robe she kept at the foot of the bed and donned slippers. They ran to the room next door.

Carol lay in her bed curled into a fetal position. "Mommy, Daddy," she cried when she saw them. "Tummy hurts."

Johnny, in the bed across from hers, looked on guiltily.

"Oh, no. She must've caught the stomach bug," John said.

Alicia, glad to be able to take her mind off her nightmare, comforted her daughter. "It's okay, honey. Do you need the bucket?" Even though Johnny seemed to have recovered from his bout, they'd let him keep the plastic basin by his bed.

"Dunno."

Alicia placed her hand on Carol's brow. "It's hot, John. Can you get the thermometer?"

He went to the bathroom and returned with it. He also brought the bucket over.

After Alicia took Carol's temperature, she said, "It's 100.4. She's sick."

"Me give her?" Johnny asked in a low voice.

"Maybe, but it's not your fault," John said. Alicia knew he didn't want his son to feel responsible.

Carol didn't throw up, so Alicia gave her something the pediatrician had recommended to settle her stomach. She and John stayed in the room until both kids fell back asleep.

"Maybe I should stay the rest of the night," Alicia offered, indicating the chair by the door where she could watch over them.

"I don't think that's necessary, hon. We're right next door. We can hear them if they wake up again."

Alicia nodded and followed John back to their bedroom. When they were both in bed again, John asked, "What were you dreaming? You were screaming louder than Carol."

Alicia didn't want to share the details of the nightmare. "I can't remember. It must've been scary, though."

John switched off the light. "Try to get some rest, and sweet dreams this time." He kissed her again and turned over.

Alicia lay with her eyes closed for a long time, remembering what her subconscious had fashioned into a bad dream. *What did it mean? Who was the figure in black?*

***

Alicia slept fitfully but had no more dreams. When she woke the next morning, John was already up making eggs. As she entered the kitchen, he was at the stove flipping an omelet.

"Mmm. That smells good, John, but I usually cook on the weekends."

"You had a tough night. I figured you could use a break. I hope Carol and Johnny are up to eating today."

"I peeked in on them when I passed the nursery. They're still sleeping, but I can wake them."

John slid the omelet onto a plate and brought it to the table next to two mugs of steaming coffee that were already there. "Not yet. Let's have a leisurely breakfast together. There's something I want to say." He got another plate and brought the silverware to the table. Dividing the omelet with a knife, he cut himself a piece and sat down across from her.

"Uh, oh. What do you want, Mr. McKinney?"

He grinned. "No, I'm not buttering you up for anything. I just want to apologize for how harsh I was last night about you and Gilly."

Alicia added a dab of milk to her coffee and took a sip. The warm liquid felt good sliding down her throat. She was amazed he would time the coffee for the exact moment she'd awaken. "I understand, John. You're worried about me."

He reached out and took her hand. "I am, Ali. I know you promised me that you wouldn't let Gilly lead you into danger, but I know how much your friendship with her means to you."

"It means a lot, John, but not as much as you and the kids. Speaking of which, I think I hear them getting up." The chatter of small voices had started from upstairs.

"I'll get them, but I don't think it's a good idea they come with us to church today. It's only twenty degrees outside, and they're just getting over a virus."

"Why don't you go, John? I'll stay here and watch them." Alicia knew he hardly ever missed Sunday services.

"Well, I do want to say some prayers for Andy. Remember, the memorial service is tonight."

"Have you spoken with him?" Alicia hadn't told John she'd gone to see him with Gilly.

"I don't know if he'll be at church but, if he isn't, I'd like to drop by and see him afterwards. I don't want to spend too much time away from you, though. I'll check Carol's temperature before I leave. If either of them gets sick, you can always text or call me on my cell. I'll have it on mute during services, but I'll check it after." He got up from his seat to get the kids, but they were already ambling down the stairs.

"Hey, good morning," Alicia said, taking Carol's hand as John took Johnny's. They walked them into the kitchen. "How are you two feeling?"

"Hungwy," Carol said. Johnny licked his lips.

Alicia laughed. "That's a good sign." She felt their foreheads. They were cool. "I think they're all better, John."

John lifted them each into their high chairs. "Excellent, but it's still too cold for them to go outside." Alicia also knew they could be antsy at church.

"Daddy's going to go out after breakfast, but I'll be here to keep you company until he comes home," she told them.

John went back to the stove and began cooking another omelet. Alicia got the orange juice pitcher out of the refrigerator and poured the kids each a glass.

"Vitamin C, good for you." Carol said, "All betta, Mommy."

"I'm glad, honey." She just hoped she and John hadn't caught the bug, but she felt okay except for a lingering feeling of dread from the memory of her nightmare.

***

After John left, she asked the twins, "Okay, guys. What do you want to do with Mommy this morning?"

Johnny said in a low voice, "I dunno." His sister said, "Stowry."

Alicia wondered if her daughter would grow up to be a librarian and author like herself. Although she couldn't yet read, she loved books.

"Okay. We can go back upstairs, and you can each choose a book for me to read from your library." She'd made sure the nursery was stocked with picture books, some of them borrowed but many more purchased.

Johnny didn't seem as enthused as Carol as they climbed the stairs next to their mother. She knew he would prefer watching cartoons on TV, a habit John didn't dissuade him from, but one she discouraged. She'd watched cartoons herself as a child but spent way more time with her head in a book, her mind transported to other times and places.

In the nursery, she pulled over a stool, so Johnny and Carol could reach the highest shelf of the bookcase, although it reached only to her waist. She waited while they browsed through the colorful covers. She realized that, for kids under five, books were indeed judged by their covers.

Johnny pulled out *The Little Engine that Could*. He pointed to the train on the cover. "Mommy wead."

Alicia smiled and took the book. She placed it next to the rocker. "How about you, young lady?"

Carol was still looking. She reminded Alicia of herself who always had a difficult time making decisions. Finally, she pulled out a book and handed it to Alicia.

Alicia laughed. She recalled Gilly had given the twins the book for Christmas. It was slightly outside their age range, an older picture book about weddings. She and John had not yet read it to the kids.

"Ladies first, I guess," she said as they joined her by the rocker. "I'll read Carol's book first. *The Wedding Party*." Johnny didn't seem upset that he had to wait for his choice, but while she read, he sucked his thumb, a habit he'd recently picked up when he was bored.

As Alicia turned the pages of the book and spoke in her librarian/author/mother read-aloud-voice, she displayed the pictures to her young audience. She also asked them questions to see if they were understanding the story. One of the pages featured a group of people attending a wedding. The bride was easy to identify in her white gown with the groom in his dark suit next to her. Carol called the ladies in pink the maids, and Alicia corrected her that they were bridesmaids. More difficult were the people dressed in regular clothing. Alicia pointed to the picture of an older woman on the bride's side. "Who do you think this is?" she asked.

The pictures were labelled underneath, but the kids couldn't yet read the words. Johnny said, "You." Alicia laughed. "I think you mean 'mother,' Johnny. That's the mother of the bride." She realized he was listening to the story even though he kept glancing away, sucking his thumb.

As Alicia continued, asking the kids to identify each person in the book including the little flower girl who Carol was so excited about that she asked if she could be one. "I'm afraid we haven't had any weddings in Cobble Cove, honey."

"Aunt Gillee?" she asked, reminding Alicia that her friend's elopement hadn't been celebrated yet. She hoped, once Kevin's killer was caught, that they could reschedule the party.

"Wead twain book," Johnny said, having lost his patience with the current story.

Alicia was about to pick up *The Little Engine That Could* when a sense of déjà vu hit her. Something nagged at the back of her mind. Then it came to her: the illustration of the wedding party brought back the strange feeling she'd had while looking at the photo of Sheila's wedding.

"Mommy, ok?" Carol asked.

"Yes, I'm fine." She reached out and took the book Johnny had chosen, but she couldn't shake the feeling she had after reading the other.

Chapter Twenty-Two

Alicia ended up reading several more books, most of them chosen by Carol. After she'd finished the fifth book, both kids had fallen asleep on the floor. They weren't taking afternoon naps anymore, but they hadn't slept well the night before so were probably making up for it.

Alicia brought the blankets from their beds and covered them. She had no idea how long they would nap but, checking the nursery's clock, she realized the church service was already over. John would be headed to Andy's house. She hoped John's newspaper intern wouldn't say anything about her and Gilly visiting him. She should've told John when she made the promise not to investigate anymore with Gilly.

As she got off the rocker, there was a knock on the front door. She left the kids and went to open it. Her father-in-law, Mac, stood on the step with Fido at his side. "Mornin', Alicia. I was out walking and thought I'd drop by. Is John around?"

"He went to church and then to see Andy. I stayed home because the kids were sick yesterday. They're fine now, but it's very cold out. I just read them some stories, and they fell asleep."

He smiled as he entered. She noticed Fido had some snow in his fur that Mac brushed off. "I'll wait for John if you don't mind. I went to the early service. Betty and I like to get an early start to the day. She's at her yoga class."

Alicia had to give her father-in-law's girlfriend and the director of the library credit for being so active in her mid-eighties. "The kids are upstairs in the nursery. Would you like some coffee or tea?"

"Don't bother." He tapped his cane as he followed Alicia into the living room.

It was then that the phone rang. Alicia wasn't used to getting calls on the house phone. Most people called her cell, but she was glad it came on that line because her cell phone was still upstairs.

She answered it, thinking it was John. "Hello?"

"Alicia, I was hoping you were home. Can you come to the inn?"

"I don't think so, Gilly. Carol was sick last night, and John isn't here . . ."

Mac, overhearing the conversation said, "Don't I count for something? Go see your friend. I'd love to stay and watch my grandkids."

Alicia hesitated. She knew John didn't like leaving Mac alone with Carol and Johnny because of his increasing memory lapses, but he would most likely be home soon, and she wouldn't spend much time at the inn.

"Okay," she said to the phone and Mac. "I'll be right over, but I can't stay long."

"This won't take much time," Gilly said. "See ya." She hung up.

Alicia worried that she was being summoned to the inn because Gilly had another clue she wanted to share. After her talk with John, she knew she couldn't get involved.

"Thanks, Mac. Should I bring the twins downstairs? I was reading to them before you came, and they fell asleep."

Mac grinned, showing the dimple John inherited from him. "I can manage the stairs, Alicia, and I can tell them some stories if they wake up. I don't need any books. Just my imagination perking in here." He touched the side of his head with his free hand. He then turned, gripped his cane, and headed up.

***

When Alicia arrived at the inn, she hadn't expected to see Mrs. Burke loading up her Oldsmobile out front, but she wasn't surprised the woman was leaving Cobble Cove. She was sure she'd seen the headlines about Sheila and Kevin.

"Mrs. McKinney," the old woman said as she tossed a suitcase into the trunk. Alicia noticed she was wearing a long coat with deep pockets and a dark scarf around her head to guard against the cold. Her tote bag of yarn and knitting needles was strung on her shoulder. "I'm glad you came. I wanted a chance to say goodbye."

"Gilly called me. I guess that's why. I'm sorry we didn't get much of a chance to get to know one another."

"I feel the same, but it's time to move on."

"Where are you headed now?"

Instead of answering, Mrs. Burke looked toward the inn door that had opened. Gilly stood there with her son Billy behind her. Billy was Gilly's youngest boy. He had just turned nine. In his arms, he held something that Alicia couldn't identify. She thought it might be a toy.

Gilly and Billy joined Alicia and Mrs. Burke by the car. Alicia now realized that Billy was holding KittyKai. The kitten seemed comfortable in his arms and wasn't protesting being carried.

"Hi, Alicia. Glad you could make it. I'm going to visit Sheila and thought you might want to come along. Billy's coming with us because his brothers are still on their sleepovers, and Edith and Rose are off today."

"What about Ramsay?"

"He got his warrant and is searching Mrs. Kleisman's house with his officers."

Alicia recalled their visit to Mrs. Kleisman the night before and how, despite her admitting she owned a gun, she appeared innocent. Still, it was possible Ramsay would uncover something on his forage through the garbage in the woman's house.

Billy said, "I'm bringing KittyKai to Mrs. Whitehead's house. Mom thinks she will cheer her up."

Alicia walked over to the boy and petted the calico's soft head. "That's a nice idea, Billy." The boy beamed. "I didn't want to leave her alone. Will Sneaky be visiting us again soon?"

"Maybe, or KittyKai might be invited to the library." Alicia knew that when Sheila returned to work she might consider KittyKai as a special guest at Sneaky story time, and Laura would be thrilled with the idea.

"If you want to come with us, we're going in Cecelia's car," Gilly said. "She's already checked out, but she wanted to finally meet Sheila before she leaves town. She offered to ride us to her house and then drop us back here after our visit."

"Does Sheila know we're all going?" Alicia asked.

"Yes. I called her before I called you. She wanted to make us brunch, but I told her not to go to any trouble. Ron should be back in a little while, and I don't want to hold Cecelia up from her travels. Sunday traffic can be rough."

"I can't be gone long either," Alicia said as Mrs. Burke opened the passenger side door for her. She and Gilly got in the back. Mrs. Burke invited Billy to sit up front with her. "Just be careful with that cat, young man. Hold him still on your lap. I don't want him attacking me while I drive."

Billy said, "Oh, don't worry, Mrs. Burke. She's a very gentle cat. I don't even need to keep her in a cat carrier when she goes anywhere."

Alicia didn't think keeping the kitten unrestrained was a great idea, but she had to admit that KittyKai was quite calm. After all, the cat had travelled all the way from Hawaii to come live with Gilly and her family here in Cobble Cove.

***

When they arrived at Sheila's house, Alicia and Gilly got out first. Mrs. Burke and Billy, holding tight to KittyKai, followed them up the walk. Before Gilly could knock, Sheila came to the door. She wore dark slacks and a buttercup sweater. A yellow headband restrained her red curls.

"Good morning, or should I say 'afternoon?' It's nearly twelve."

"Hi, Sheila. You're looking well," Gilly said.

"I'm feeling fine, thank you. Please come in . . . all of you."

The four followed in a line into Sheila's cheerful living room. Mrs. Burke had dropped behind Billy and closed the door once everyone was inside.

"Have a seat," Sheila said. "Can I get any of you anything?"

"We're only here for a short visit," Gilly said. "Billy brought KittyKai to cheer you up, and I brought my guest, Cecelia Burke. She wanted to meet you since she's leaving Cobble Cove today."

As Mrs. Burke stepped forward, Alicia had that déjà vu feeling again. Her eyes darted to Sheila's wedding photo. Suddenly, she realized what it was that had bothered her about it. The woman standing next to Sheila's husband in the picture was a younger version of Cecelia.

Mrs. Burke lowered her scarf. "Hello, Sheila. We finally meet."

Sheila's face paled. "Oh, my God. It can't be . . . Lucille." She backed away. At the same time, Mrs. Burke withdrew a pistol from her pocket. "I'm afraid it is. My chocolates didn't work, but I think bullets are more effective. At least they were for Kevin."

Alicia gasped. Gilly said, "What's going on? Who are you?"

Still pointing the gun at Sheila, Mrs. Burke replied, "I'm Lucille Whitehead, the mother of the man she murdered."

Chapter Twenty-Three

"Lucille. No. I didn't harm Tom. I loved him. You can't blame me after all these years."

"I can, and I do." As she cocked back the gun's trigger, KittyKai let out a yowl. Jumping from Billy's grasp, she launched herself at Cecelia, landing on her arm. The woman dropped the gun in surprise and pain as she rolled up her sleeve to check for a scratch. Alicia ran toward the gun and picked it up. "Stay where you are, Mrs. Whitehead."

Gilly took out her cell. "I'm calling my husband. He'll be here to arrest you."

Alicia had never fired a gun, but she hoped Lucille wouldn't realize that.

Sheila's mother-in-law smiled. It was a chilling sight that reminded Alicia of another madwoman she'd encountered in the past. "Your husband is too busy chasing false clues. I was at that chocolate making class under an alias." She kicked KittyKai away. The kitten scurried back to Billy who ran forward to get her. Gilly screamed, "No, Billy. Stay here," but it was too late. Cecelia caught the boy and withdrew a needle from her tote bag. Alicia saw it wasn't a knitting needle. It was a syringe.

Lucille held it against Billy's neck. "You'll step away and let me out, or I'll inject this child with the same concoction I inserted into those chocolates, but at a much higher dosage."

"You leave my son alone," Gilly said. She was about to rush forward when Alicia held her back. "Don't, Gilly. You can't chance it." Billy stood there frozen, his eyes wide.

Sheila looked horrified. Alicia wished she could shoot Billy's captor in the leg, but without any experience shooting a gun, she couldn't risk it.

The three women backed away as Lucille walked slowly toward the door, holding Billy against her. "Come with me, Tommy," she said in a high-pitched voice that sounded younger. We're going for a little ride and don't want to be late."

"My God," Sheila said in a hushed voice. "She thinks Billy is Tommy."

Gilly whispered to Alicia, "As soon as she gets in that car, I'm calling Ron. He'll catch her before she reaches the highway."

Lucille shoved Billy in the passenger side where he'd sat previously. She slid in next to him and locked the doors. Stomping on the gas, she sped away.

The three women stood in the doorway looking on in horror. Gilly called Ramsay. "Ron, Cecelia Burke's real name is Lucille Whitehead, she's Sheila's mother in law. She tried to shoot Sheila and took Billy. She's in a blue 2005 Oldsmobile. I'm sorry I didn't get the plate number. She just left Sheila's house. You have to stop her. Hurry." Tears started to roll down Gilly's cheeks. Alicia, placing the gun down, put an arm around her. "It'll be okay, Gilly. Ramsay will catch her."

Sheila said, "This is all my fault. I should've known she'd do this one day."

Gilly suddenly broke free of Alicia's embrace. "Wait." Her sobs subsided, and her face lit up with the determination Alicia was used to seeing in her friend. She turned to Sheila. "Give me your car keys. I don't have to wait for Ron." She picked up the gun Alicia had dropped. "Are you coming with me, Alicia?"

She thought of John's warning and her promise to him. "No. I'm sorry. I can't, and you shouldn't either." She looked toward Sheila. "Don't give her your keys. Let the police do their jobs. They're trained professionals."

"Alicia's right," Sheila said. "I know how hard it is to give up control, but sometimes it's necessary."

Alicia thought of the time her own kids were in jeopardy. How she and John had made a move that had nearly cost them their lives. "Stay here with us, Gilly. They can't get far."

"And Lucille won't endanger Billy. You heard her call him Tommy. It's me she wants."

Gilly sighed and laid down the gun. "I can't fire that, anyway. I've been after Ron to teach me."

"I should call John," Alicia said. "Maybe he can get a special edition of the paper out with Billy and Mrs. Burke's photos, so people can identify them and contact the police." But just as she took out her cell, a car pulled up with two people in it. She recognized Ryan but not the dark-haired young woman with him. Sheila let out a cry and ran to them.

Alicia and Gilly watched as the young woman got out of the car. She and Sheila embraced. "Julie, I thought you were coming tomorrow."

"I managed an earlier flight, Mom. I wanted to surprise you. I called Ryan, and he picked me up at the airport. Are you okay? You look upset."

"I'm alright, Julie, but there's been an incident. Come in and get settled, and I'll explain."

Ryan kissed Sheila's cheek. "Is there something I can do to help?" He looked toward Gilly and Alicia. "Why are your friends here and . . . what's that gun doing there?"

"Just come in, please. I have a lot of explaining to do to you all."

Sheila made some quick introductions of her daughter to Gilly and Alicia and then everyone went back inside the house. In the commotion, Alicia realized they'd forgotten about KittyKai, who was rolled up scared and small in the corner where Mrs. Burke had kicked her. She picked the kitten up. "I hope KittyKai isn't hurt. Maybe she needs to go to a vet."

"Let me have her," Gilly said. She reached out and took the kitten in her arms. Stroking her gently, she murmured, "It's okay, KittyKai. You're safe. That bad lady isn't going to hurt you anymore." When the kitten began to purr, tears began to slide down Gilly's cheeks.

"Sit down, all of you, please," Sheila said. "I'll make coffee and then I'll fill everyone in on what happened here a few moments ago. By then, I'm hoping Ramsay will have caught my mother-in-law."

"Your mother-in-law?" Ryan raised an eyebrow in puzzlement.

"Let me help you with the coffee," Gilly said, wiping her tears with her coat sleeve. "I have to do something to keep my mind off . . ." Her voice choked as she handed Alicia back the kitten. "Watch KittyKai while I help Sheila. I think she's okay."

Alicia took the purring calico and sat on the couch between Julie and Ryan. When Sheila returned and laid out the coffee with some cookies that no one touched, she took a chair facing them. Gilly remained standing on the other side of her, ironically in front of the photo that featured a younger Mrs. Whitehead in Sheila's wedding party. Gilly had taken KittyKai back and was stroking the kitten as she listened to Sheila's story. She seemed calmer now but held the cat like a baby, pacing with it as Alicia used to do to quiet Johnny and Carol. It was obvious she was fighting hard to control herself.

"You never knew your father's mother," Sheila began addressing Julie. "There was a reason for that." She paused. "When I met Tom, I had no idea his mother was obsessed with her only child, although I should've suspected something. We met in Syracuse when I went away to college. Tom was boarding there, too. He was a wonderful man, and I loved him dearly." Her voice turned wistful. "He told me his family came from New Jersey and that he'd decided to go away to school to escape his overprotective mother. I thought he was exaggerating because most young men are seeking their independence at that age. But when I met his parents, I realized that, while his father was a similarly kind and gentle man, his mother was emotionally unbalanced. I later learned, after we married, that her disorder worsened when Tom moved away with me to Cobble Cove to the home my parents had left me. Lucille was a nurse which was ironic because she didn't recognize her own illness. She thought her obsession with her son was perfectly normal. Tom's dad confided in me that his wife had lost several babies prior to Tom's birth and maybe that was part of the reason she became so protective of him." She took a breath as everyone listened to her tale. Even Gilly stopped pacing.

"You all know that I lost my husband very early in my marriage. Julie, you were just a baby and don't remember your father. When he died, Lucille went even further off the edge. She blamed me. She accused me of not having him see a doctor, but he had no symptoms, at least none he shared with me. Then she went as far as saying that I'd done something to him to cause the aneurysm. As a nurse, she should've known better. I got calls from her threatening me. Ted, my father-in-law, tried to help. He took her to a psychiatrist. She only went to one session and then refused to continue. I thought I could deal with her another way, so I invited her to our house. I had a heart-to-heart talk with her. I thought that would solve things, but she was sicker than I realized." Sheila took another deep breath. "She attacked me with a knife. Luckily, I was able to subdue her. I should've called the police, but I didn't. When I told Ted Whitehead what had happened, he was horrified. He promised me that he'd make sure she wouldn't bother me again. That was the last I heard from them. I should've known that she'd come back for me one day."

Alicia was putting it all together. "Lucille said her husband died recently. That's probably when she decided to seek her revenge."

"Yes," Sheila said. "Burke was Lucille's maiden name. I should've recognized it, but I don't believe you mentioned it more than once, and I wasn't paying much attention. It's been more than twenty-five years." She looked toward the wedding photo.

"A long time to hold a grudge," Ryan said.

"She called Billy 'Tommy'," Gilly pointed out.

"Yes. That's why I'm hopeful she won't harm him. She may be imagining he's her son as a boy."

Before any of the others could voice their opinions, a police car pulled up outside. John's car was right behind it. Ramsay rushed up the walk with John following him. Gilly opened the door to the two men.

"Ron," she cried, falling into his arms. "Did you find them?"

His face red, the sheriff shook his head. "I'm sorry, Abby. There was a bad accident on the highway. It blocked things off. I tried to get around it. By the time I did, she must've gotten a head start. I have all my men out there, though, and have alerted the nearby police districts including Detective Stryder in Carlsville. I texted everyone Billy's photo. They won't get far."

Alicia recalled Detective Stryder who'd worked on her and John's own kidnapping case, and although he hadn't caught the person who'd taken the twins, his expertise was instrumental in solving the case.

John said, "Honey, Ramsay contacted me with the news, and I hurried here. I called Dad, and he'll stay longer to watch the twins. Betty's joining him at the house after her yoga class. Are you okay?"

"I'm fine, but I feel so helpless. There must be something I can do."

Ramsay glanced around the room at those gathered. "I think you should all go home and sit tight. I'll update everyone as I receive further news."

"I'm not going anywhere," Gilly said. "The boys aren't coming home until tonight, and Edith and Rose can take care of the inn until then."

"I'm staying around, too," Ryan said. Julie added, "I was hoping to stay with Mom, anyway. My bags are in Professor Anderson's car."

"Of course, you can stay," Sheila said. She looked around to include the others. "All of you."

Alicia recognized the turn of Ramsay's lips as a partial pout. Her husband and son were both good at making them. "Only the family members can stay." He turned to her and John. "The McKinneys should go home. I'll bring Abby back to the inn. Our boys will be home soon, and I need to be there to break the news to them."

Alicia saw Gilly's tear-stained eyes light up when the sheriff used the word "our" to include her sons.

Ryan stepped forward. "I'm not exactly a family member, but I'm staying, too. Will you have officers watching this house?"

"If Sheila permits it."

Sheila sighed. Alicia knew it was an effort for her to give up control, but she also knew that Sheila realized that if she hadn't sent away Ramsay's men, her mother-in-law may have been caught, and Billy Nostran would still be here with his mother. "Okay. Let me know if there's anything else I can do."

Ramsay waved his arm. "Just sit tight. If you get a call from Whitehead, alert us right away. I'll need to take your cell phone in case it comes in on that. As I said before, I've consulted with Stryder. He's an expert in these matters, and he tells me we should expect a call within the next few hours asking for the ransom and where to bring it."

"Ransom? Oh, no." Sheila shook her head so violently that her headband nearly jerked off. "There won't be any ransom. Lucille isn't after money. She wants revenge on me. The only ransom she'll demand is my life."

Alicia recalled how Lucille had bribed Tucker into delivering the laced chocolates with the promise of a big payback. She also remembered the woman saying she was a rich widow. Perhaps Sheila was right, and unlike the ransom demanded of her and John two winters ago, Lucille wasn't after money.

Ryan placed an arm lightly on Sheila as if to steady her. "I don't have any experience with kidnappings, but I have an idea this may play out differently. I heard you say that your mother-in-law called Billy by your husband's name. You might be right that she, in her disturbed state, believes that she's taken her son back."

At Ryan's words, Alicia saw Gilly's face pale. If what he said was true, there might not be a call after all. Lucille might decide to escape with the boy she lost years ago, the boy she believed Sheila had stolen from her.

Chapter Twenty-Four

Not putting much weight on Ryan's theory, Ramsay gave Sheila, her daughter, and the professor further instructions on what to do if Mrs. Burke contacted them. As he left with Gilly who held tight to KittyKai, an unmarked car pulled up with two of his men. He spoke to them a few minutes and then helped his wife into his patrol car. Alicia, having given Gilly a last hug and assuring her that all would be okay although she herself wasn't too confident about that, got into John's car.

After Alicia picked up her own car at the inn, she drove home behind John. They met in the driveway.

"Before we go in," Alicia said, "What should we tell Mac and Betty?"

"The truth. There's no sense in hiding anything from them, although Ramsay told me not to publish the news yet. Stryder advised him to keep it quiet until they hear from Mrs. Whitehead."

Alicia was surprised. She thought running the story in the *Courier* would help people report any sightings of Sheila's mother-in-law and Billy.

"What if Lucille doesn't call? What if Ryan's right, and she just decides to keep Billy as her revenge?" The thought sent shudders up Alicia's spine.

"That won't happen, honey. She may be crazy, but her real incentive is to kill Sheila. Let's go inside and talk more about this later. The police are doing everything they can. She can't get far with New Jersey plates, and she doesn't know the area. Besides, Billy is a smart boy. He may figure out a way to escape."

"I don't know, John. This brings back the terrible memory of what happened with the twins."

He hung his head. "I know, but they were babies. Billy is nine years old. He can protect himself from an old woman."

Alicia sighed. "I hope so. I feel so awful for Gilly. I wish I could help her."

"That's Ramsay and his men's jobs. C'mon." He placed an arm around her, and they walked to the door as Betty opened it.

***

Mac and Betty took the news calmly. In their eighty-plus years they'd faced many dramas and had learned to be strong. Mac had lost his wife to a lengthy battle with cancer, and Betty's husband and children had been gunned down by a Manhattan mugger.

"We can stay here longer if you'd like," Betty offered. "I know you'd want to be with your friend at a time like this, and John might want to be with Sheila."

"No," John said. "Thanks, but there's nothing we can do. Sheila has Ryan and her daughter. Gilly has Ramsay."

"Alright. The twins are asleep again. Mac and I did our best to tire them out, but they also tired us out." She laughed. "Thank goodness I'm keeping up with my yoga."

"My grandchildren sure are feisty," Mac agreed.

John grinned. "I take it they've recovered from their tummy aches."

"Oh, yes. They both had an early lunch. I made them some homemade chicken soup. There's more in a plastic container in the refrigerator if you two want any."

"Thanks so much, Betty and you, too, Mac." Alicia walked them to the door, their canes tapping the floor in rhythm to their steps. Fido, who'd also been exhausted by the toddlers and was sleeping in the corner, had to be prodded by John to follow his owners.

When they were gone, Alicia and John went upstairs and checked on the twins. They were both curled up sleeping in their beds, their bedcovers tucked in around them.

"They look so peaceful, John. I know what Gilly must be going through."

"We can't let them sleep all day, and Gilly is stronger than you give her credit for. Remember, she survived her divorce and raising those three kids alone."

Alicia knew he was right, but her heart still ached at the knowledge her friend's son was in the company of a madwoman.

***

They ended up taking Betty's offer and eating some of her homemade soup before waking the kids. Alicia found she had more of an appetite than she expected since she hadn't eaten since early in the morning. John licked his bowl clean. "Betty makes as good a soup as my mom used to," he said. "No wonder Dad is so charmed by her."

"I know I didn't charm you with my cooking." While Alicia could put together a decent meal, she didn't consider herself on the level of John and his family unless she considered his sister Pamela who ate out most of the time.

"You had other charms, Ali." He put his spoon in his empty bowl and took her hand, dropping his voice as he looked into her eyes. "I know how worried you must be about Gilly, but Ramsay will catch Mrs. Whitehead."

Alicia prayed he was right. "What about Kevin Tucker's memorial tonight? Are you going? Should I stay here with the twins?"

He kept his hand on hers. It was as warm as his voice. "I promised Andy I'd be there. You should come with me. I'm sure Dad and Betty won't mind coming back tonight to watch Johnny and Carol. We don't have to stay there long."

Alicia nodded. "Okay. I'll come."

***

Alicia tried to take her mind off Gilly and Sheila's situations the rest of the afternoon. She and John watched cartoons with the kids, played some indoor games with them including hide and seek and Simon Says. They avoided taking them out, even though Johnny wanted to go to the children's museum again. Alicia made the excuse they were just getting over their stomach viruses and couldn't afford a relapse. With a kidnapper in the area, the last thing she wanted was for the twins to be snatched again.

When Mac and Betty showed up without Fido, Alicia thanked them again and promised not to be late at the memorial.

"Don't worry, dear," Betty said. "I know it's important that you and John pay your respects, and we enjoy spending time with your children."

Despite the sincerity of her voice, Alicia knew it wasn't easy to manage twin toddlers.

***

As they drove to the funeral home, Alicia gazed out the car window at the dark winter night, wondering about Billy and if he was being fed and kept warm.

John read her thoughts. "He's okay, Ali. Mrs. Whitehead won't harm him. She just needs him to get to Sheila."

"Then why hasn't she called yet? What is she waiting for? They could be miles away by now."

John turned into the full parking lot of the funeral parlor. "I doubt that. I say she's still in town."

"If that's so, then why hasn't anyone reported seeing her and Billy or spotted their car?"

He parked in the one empty space at the far end of the lot. "Sorry, we have to walk a bit. I can't answer your questions, Ali. Try to relax. I know it isn't easy, but sometimes we have to let things go."

The meditation tapes she'd gotten him for Christmas seemed to be working, Alicia reflected as John got out of the car and came around to her side to help her out. She considered borrowing them. She couldn't keep her nerves under control while her peaceful Cobble Cove was in a state of turmoil again.

As they approached the door, Alicia saw it was flanked by two uniformed policemen. Three patrol cars were parked out front. "John, is this normal for a memorial service?"

He nodded. "I would imagine, yes, since it's for a murder victim."

Alicia thought about the mystery books she read and the ones she and John wrote where the killers often showed up at their victims' funerals. Was Ramsay counting on the fact Lucille would turn up here? But, if she did, what about Billy?

They walked in from the cold February night into the stifling heat of the funeral home. The cloying smell of flowers and sweating people assaulted her nostrils. The place was packed. She found it hard to breathe and opened her coat. John, sensing her discomfort, placed an arm around her. "Relax, Ali. We won't be here long."

Besides the sitting area, there was only one room in the home, which was used for services. As they entered, John signed the guest book by the door. Alicia saw Andy up front by the closed casket, Kim by his side. They were surrounded by several town residents. She recognized Sheila and Gilly, both dressed in black, and was surprised to see them there.

"I thought Sheila would stay at her house with her daughter and Ryan," Alicia whispered to John, "and wasn't Gilly staying at the inn?"

"You know Sheila," John whispered back, "She wouldn't miss this especially since she feels she was responsible. As for Gilly, I'm guessing Ramsay couldn't keep her home but made sure there was plenty of police presence here to protect her."

Since Kevin had no family in Cobble Cove and the only relatives living elsewhere were either in jail or incommunicado with him, Andy had arranged and paid for the service.

As she and John moved forward, careful not to bump shoulders with any of the guests, Alicia saw Ryan and Julie sitting in the front row. They were both keeping a close eye on Sheila.

Alicia walked over to Andy. She wasn't sure what to say. "Andy, we're so sorry." He turned to her, his eyes red-rimmed. "Thank you for coming." John shook his hand and gave him a pat on the back. It was then that the pastor entered. "Please have a seat, everyone. The service is about to begin."

Sheila, smiling weakly at Alicia, sat in the seat between Ryan and Julie. Gilly beckoned Alicia and John to sit next to her and Ramsay. Andy and Kim sat at the end of the aisle.

The pastor began with a prayer and then spoke a few words. After her short speech, she invited people up to share their memories about Kevin. Andy walked to the front of the room and faced everyone. "Kevin Tucker was my friend," he said in a quivering voice. "He messed up his life at one point, and we grew apart. Then he decided to change his ways. He started his own courier business and was hoping to go back to school with the money he was saving." He paused and wiped a tear from his eyes with a handkerchief he took from his suit pocket. "Those plans were dashed when he was murdered. Sheriff Ramsay is currently searching for the person responsible for that act. She calls herself Cecelia Burke, but we know her real name is Lucille Whitehead." There were murmurs throughout the room. Alicia hadn't expected Andy to talk so freely about the investigation, but maybe he thought it would help people come forward with information.

"There are signs around town," Andy continued. "If anyone has seen Billy Nostran or Lucille Whitehead, please contact Sheriff Ramsay." He looked toward Ramsay and Gilly and was about to walk back to his seat when the door burst open, and a heavy woman rushed through. Everyone turned, and Alicia was shocked to see it was Rhonda Kleisman.

"I know where they are," she said, catching her breath. "They're in my house."

Chapter Twenty-Five

There was much commotion after Mrs. Kleisman's announcement. Ramsay took her aside and, after questioning her, told his wife, "Take the car home, honey. I'll be going with my men here to the Kleismans'."

Gilly said, "I'm going with you, Ron. If Billy is in that house with that woman, I want to be there."

"No. It's too dangerous." He spoke to John. "Can you and Alicia take her to your house? I'll update you as soon as we see what's going on."

John nodded. "No problem. We'll keep an eye on her." Gilly didn't seem appeased, but she relented.

"Do you need me?" Sheila asked. "I know I'm the one she's after."

"Mom, don't." Julie put an arm on her as if to hold her back.

Ryan said, "There's no need for you to be involved. Let the police handle this, Sheila."

Ramsay agreed. "You all go home. I'll be in touch."

As Alicia and John walked Gilly to their car, Alicia wondered how Lucille had ended up in Kleisman's house. She recalled that they'd taken the chocolate-making class at Cocoa Cocoa. Could she, not knowing anyone else in town, have asked Mrs. Kleisman to shelter her until she made whatever move she was planning next?

"It doesn't make sense," Gilly said as they were driving. "Why would Mrs. Kleisman help Sheila's mother-in-law? And what about her children? Why would she leave them alone with her? Couldn't she have just called the police instead of making that grand entrance at Kevin's wake?"

"She must've had her reasons," John said. "I'm sure Ramsay will fill us in as soon as they have all the information."

"I hope he doesn't put himself in danger," Gilly said. Alicia noticed she was gripping her hands in her lap.

"He'll be fine. He's taking several armed officers with him. Remember, Whitehead lost her gun. All she has are some needles."

Gilly nodded, and it seemed to Alicia that she was trying to believe John's statement. "I wish I could be there. Billy must be so scared."

"Try not to worry. I've been through this, and it doesn't help." Alicia knew her words wouldn't do much to calm Gilly's fears.

***

They heard sooner than Alicia expected. Ramsay arrived at their house less than a half hour later to pick up his wife. Gilly ran to the door. Alicia saw her stop and cry out, "Where's Billy? Oh, God, you didn't get him."

Ramsay, his face grim, put his arms around his wife. "I'm sorry, Abby. They were gone by the time we got there. I have Mrs. Kleisman in custody. I think it was a setup. The older kid claimed she was put in charge of watching Billy and Whitehead. It seems Kleisman was paid to shelter them, but she changed her mind thinking there was some bigger reward she'd receive for letting the police know. She made up a story about going shopping while she went to the funeral home. Meanwhile, Whitehead gave Kleisman's kid more money, so she could escape with Billy."

"How awful," Alicia said, feeling their pain.

"Come have a seat, Ramsay," John offered. "This must've been a tough night for you."

Ramsay wiped a stray strand of hair off his face. His eyes looked worn and troubled. "Sure was, but I still have to break the news to Sheila." He reached into his pocket and withdrew a folded piece of loose-leaf paper. "Whitehead left this for us. It's addressed to Sheila and is the terms for her releasing Billy."

Gilly gasped. "What does it say, Ron?"

"I don't think it's necessary for you to read it."

She gave him a glare that would've made Alicia laugh if the situation wasn't so serious.

Ramsay sighed. "Very well. I'll read it aloud." He unfolded the paper. "*My Dearest Sheila, We both know why I took the boy. You once took my boy. Unfortunately, I never got him back. If you want the kid, meet me in front of the library tonight at ten p.m. Don't bring anyone with you. If I see that sheriff or any of his men, I'll take Tommy away forever.*"

Gilly's face paled at the words. "What are you going to do, Ron? You can't send Sheila there by herself."

Ramsay nodded. "I don't intend to. All kidnappers say the same thing. I've been in touch with Stryder. He's the expert in this area, and he's on his way here to help." He checked his watch. "It's eight o'clock. We have two hours. She must be hiding somewhere during that time. It's freezing out tonight, so she must be indoors somewhere. I'm sending my officers around town to check out places. If we're lucky, we'll find her before she reaches the library."

"What about Sheila?" Alicia wanted to know. "If you don't catch Lucille by ten, are you sending her to the library?"

"I'm consulting Stryder about that. We very well may need to do that, but I'm sure he'll have a plan to back her up." He glanced toward the door. "As much as I hate to do this, I have to go to Sheila now. John, do you mind bringing Gilly back to the inn? I can get one of the officers to help pick up our car from the funeral home later."

Before John could answer, Gilly said, "No, Ron. I'm not going anywhere this time except to the library at ten if you don't find them. I won't stand around waiting to see what happens to Sheila and my son."

Alicia knew exactly how Gilly felt. In her case, she'd convinced John to take her along to deliver ransom money. Although that went sideways, it eventually worked out.

Ramsay must've recognized the determination in Gilly's words because he shrugged his shoulders and said, "Very well, Abby. Let's hope it doesn't get to that. I'll call with any news and be back for you at nine thirty. That is if Stryder allows it."

Gilly's voice changed from its stubborn tone to one of anger. "I don't care what Stryder says. You're the sheriff of this town, Ron, and I'm your wife."

He bowed his head in agreement. "Okay, Gilly. I'll be back to get you. . . if it comes to that."

***

The next two hours passed excruciatingly slowly. Alicia brought the twins down to amuse Gilly and raise her spirits, but she saw that they only reminded her of her three kids when they were young.

The twins' bedtime was usually eight, but they allowed them to stay up until nine that night. When it was time to take them upstairs, Alicia asked Gilly to come along with her. John stayed downstairs waiting for Ramsay's call.

"Aunt Gilly is going to read you stories tonight," Alicia said as they entered the nursery that had been converted into a bedroom for the toddlers.

That announcement was met with yaaay's and claps from Carol and Johnny. Gilly took a seat in the rocker while Alicia pulled up the other chair in the room next to her.

"I know what you're doing, Alicia, and I appreciate it, but you know I can't keep my mind off what's going on."

"I don't expect you to, Gilly, but having you put them to bed is a treat for the twins."

Gilly smiled and picked up one of the books she'd given Carol and Johnny. Thankfully, it wasn't the one about the family wedding that had tipped off Alicia about Lucille.

As Gilly read, Alicia noticed her glancing at the wall clock checking the time. The kids fell asleep at nine fifteen, and she helped Gilly carry them into their beds. Once they were tucked in, Alicia switched off the light and closed the door halfway. She and Gilly tiptoed downstairs. The timing couldn't have been more perfect. As soon as they descended, there was a tap at the door. John went to answer it. He ushered in Ramsay and Stryder. They displayed grim expressions.

The black detective who'd helped Alicia and John when the twins were kidnapped spoke first. "Hello, Mr. and Mrs. McKinney, Mrs. Ramsay."

Alicia walked to John's side; Gilly to Ramsay's. "You don't have good news for us, do you?" she asked, her voice trembling.

"I'm afraid we don't, Abby," Ramsay said.

Stryder blew out a breath of cold air. Alicia noted how he towered over the sheriff. Stepping further in the house, he said, "Sheriff Ramsay has filled me in about this case. We're setting up some men in the park next to the library while Mrs. Whitehead meets with her mother-in-law. The Sheriff and I will be in an unmarked car nearby monitoring the meet. She'll be outfitted with a comms unit, so we can hear and see everything that takes place. At any sign of trouble, we'll signal our men to go in to help."

"What about me?" Gilly asked. "I told Ron I'd go. I can't stay here and wait while my son's life is in jeopardy."

Stryder glanced toward Ramsay. "Yes, your husband gave me that request, but we can't allow it."

"Steve, I'd like you to reconsider," Ramsay said. "I'll take full responsibility for her."

Stryder sighed. "Okay. She can join us in the van."

"Thanks." Ramsay looked toward Alicia and John. "We'll be leaving now. I have officers at Sheila's house prepping her with the comms unit and a bulletproof vest."

"Bulletproof vest? Don't you still have her gun?" Gilly asked.

Ramsay glanced down at the floor. "We do, but Kleisman revealed during her interrogation at the station that Whitehead took the one she kept in her house for protection." "

Oh, my God!" Gilly exclaimed. "Sheila can wear a vest, but what about Billy?"

Chapter Twenty-Six

As Stryder, Ramsay, and Gilly began to leave, Alicia called out, "Wait! I want to come, too."

John and Stryder opened their mouths, about to object, when Alicia continued, "Gilly's my friend, and I've been through this before. I won't get in the way. I just want to be there if she needs me."

Her voice choking with emotion, Gilly said, "Please let her come."

Stryder shook his large shoulders. "Why don't we invite the whole town? But, alright, maybe they'll keep one another out of trouble."

Alicia turned to John. "You understand, don't you? Stay with the twins. I'll be back as soon as I can."

John hugged her. "I know, Ali. Stay safe, please."

***

They were in place in the park by nine thirty, a half hour before Burke and Billy were scheduled to meet Sheila. Although it was a windy night with temperatures hovering in the low twenties, it was warm inside the van. They couldn't keep the motor running, but the closeness of the four people inside provided heat, and everyone was so keyed up they didn't notice any chills.

Stryder and Ramsay sat by the camera observing the area around the library. Burke hadn't indicated exactly where she'd be, so they needed to span the front, sides, and back of the building. Sheila would be released by Ramsay's men to the entrance that was bordered by bushes that Burke could hide behind, but no movement had been detected. If she was there waiting with Billy, there was no sign of her. Stryder explained the equipment to Ramsay, but Alicia knew it was more for the benefit of her and Gilly. He said that they would be in contact with Sheila through the comms unit which was a listening device Sheila would be wearing in her ear. They would also be able to see her movements and that of Lucille's and Billy's.

"How fast can your men respond?" Gilly asked.

"They're stationed around the perimeter, Abby. As soon as Stryder or I give the word, they can be at the library in under a minute."

Alicia wondered if that made Gilly feel any better.

***

The wait seemed like forever. Alicia watched Gilly gnawing at her nails. Her friend never kept them polished, but she'd had a manicure in Hawaii, and Alicia cringed as she saw the bitten and cracked paint. The sounds from the monitor—night noises, creatures stirring in the dark, the occasional whistle of the wind—mixed with the deep breathing inside the van. Everyone was on edge. Ramsay and Stryder leaned into the monitor observing every corner of the screen. Then, just as Alicia could bear the silence no longer, two figures emerged on the street.

"Billy!" Gilly exclaimed, but Stryder put a finger against his lips. "Shhh. We have eyes on them. Ramsay will give the signal to his men for Sheila in a moment."

Alicia watched as the two bodies, the old woman hunched but determined, the young boy in step next to her, advanced toward the Cobble Cove Library statue of the boy and girl reading that stood outside the library.

"They're in place," Ramsay spoke through his mic that was connected to his head officer. "By the statue. Go ahead and give Sheila the cue. We're watching."

Alicia held her breath as, a second later, Sheila appeared on the screen approaching the statue. Her mother-in-law and Billy stood there. As Stryder zoomed in on them, they saw the gun Lucille held against Billy's head.

"No!" Gilly screamed, scrambling to the van door, but Alicia blocked her. "Let me out there. Please." Tears streamed from her eyes.

"This is what I was afraid of," Stryder muttered. Ramsay quickly went to his wife. "Calm down, Abby. We're doing everything we can. Whitehead won't hurt Billy. She wants Sheila."

Gilly crumpled in Ramsay's arms. He led her back to her seat. "Alicia, please watch her. I have to work with Stryder."

They looked on, as if transfixed by a TV drama. Sheila addressed her mother-in-law. "Lucille, listen to me. Let the boy go and take me if that's what you want."

The camera zoomed in on Lucille. She smiled. "It's not going to be that easy, Sheila. I shouldn't have let you take Tommy. I've regretted that for years."

Alicia's heart sank at the sight of Billy's wide, terror-filled eyes at what she supposed he believed were a crazy woman's words. She could only imagine the pain Gilly was experiencing and knew that was another reason Stryder and Ramsay hadn't wanted her to accompany them.

"What do you want me to do?" Sheila asked. She stood about a yard from them. "I can't bring Tom back. God knows, I've wanted to all these years. Don't you realize he meant as much to me as he did to you?" Her voice started to quiver, and Alicia imagined she was beginning to cry.

"You liar! How can that be?" Lucille tightened her grip on Billy. "You didn't give birth to him. You didn't sit by his bedside when he was sick. You never saw his first steps, heard him call you 'Momma'. All you did was turn him away from me."

Alicia realized that Sheila was getting nowhere arguing with her mother-in-law. Stryder must've understood this, too, because he whispered, "If this standoff continues, I'm sending my men in. That old woman is no match against them."

"Not yet," Ramsay cautioned staring at the screen. "You don't want her doing anything rash. She could pull that trigger by accident."

Gilly, staring almost as wide-eyed as Billy, shook her head. "My husband's right. We have to wait until she lets Billy go."

While everyone seemed to be pondering how that would be accomplished, a tall figure entered from the side of the screen. "What the—?" Stryder zoomed in, and they saw it was Ryan Anderson.

"What's the professor doing there? Didn't your men order him to stay home with Sheila's daughter?"

"Sorry, Steve, but he insisted on coming along. He promised to stay back."

"Well, I guess he broke that promise." Stryder regarded Ramsay with an angry look.

Ryan stood next to Sheila who turned at his approach. "I won't let you do this alone." He looked toward Lucille and Billy. "Sheila has come here at your request. You said you would release Billy."

"I also said she was to come alone but now that you're here, it might be fitting for you to lose the one you love, like I lost my son because of her." She raised her gun and, in that moment, Billy broke free and ran into the bushes.

Gilly screamed, but Ramsay quieted her. "It's okay. There are officers in the bushes. They'll get him."

Alicia was now more concerned with Sheila. She watched as Ryan jumped in front of her. "Go ahead. Shoot."

"That stupid man. He's not wearing a vest," Stryder said.

"Lucille wants Sheila."

"At this point, she'll kill anyone who gets in her way."

"You can't do this, Ryan," Sheila said. "Go back and leave me with her. I need to settle this myself."

Ryan didn't budge. "Did you hear me, Mrs. Whitehead? Go ahead and shoot," he challenged again.

"You better be ready to signal your men," Stryder said to Ramsay. "Billy's safe now."

"They won't get there in time," Ramsay said. "I think Ryan is trying to call her bluff."

"Stupid man," Stryder muttered again.

"I don't want to kill you," Lucille said, "but I will if you don't let me have Sheila. I want her to pay for all the years my son's been gone, for all the pain she caused me. My husband had me see a psychiatrist. He tried to convince me that I was wrong, but I knew I was right. After he died, I was all alone. If Tommy was still here, I'd have him. But, no." Her hand quivered as she waved the gun, "That woman you're protecting. She's the one who killed my boy. I seek justice for him."

"And what about Kevin Tucker? What did he do?' Ryan asked.

"That dumb kid? I knew he'd tell the cops about me when they found out he was the one who delivered my chocolates. I didn't have the money to pay him, anyway."

"He's keeping her talking. That's good," Stryder said.

"Can I go out to Billy?" Gilly asked.

"No, Abby," Ramsay said. "Everyone has to stay here. I'm sure he's in good hands now."

"You have nothing to gain from killing us," Ryan said. "It won't bring back your son, and it'll only add to your prison sentence."

Lucille continued smiling. "I don't care about that. I'm an old woman. I don't have many years left, but I want to rest in peace knowing I've avenged Tommy."

Sheila stepped next to Ryan. He tried to pull her back, but she refused to go. "Then go ahead. Kill me, but there's something you should know."

"What is she doing?" Stryder's face paled. Alicia's heart began to beat faster.

"Tom had a daughter. She's here with me tonight. She lives in California now with her own family. You have grandchildren. Tom's grandchildren."

"I don't believe you. You killed Tom only a few months after you married him."

"I didn't kill him. He died of a brain aneurysm, Lucille. I was three months pregnant with Julie. She has two daughters. One looks like you, and the other like Tom. I have a photo of them. It's on my phone." She reached into her pocket.

Lucille kept her gun extended, but her face changed. She was curious. "Throw it to me. Let me see."

"This is our chance," Stryder said. "We can move your men in, Ramsay."

"One more minute." Ramsay's eyes were locked on the screen. Sheila tossed the phone, but Lucille kicked it away.

"I know what you're trying to do, and I won't fall for it. I've had enough of your bullshit. This ends now." She stepped forward and raised the gun toward Sheila's head. Even inside the van, Alicia could hear the safety release.

Chapter Twenty-Seven

The gun failed to fire. Lucille shook it and said, "What's going on? What did that Kleisman woman do? There are no bullets in this thing."

Ryan saw the opportunity to lunge forward. He grabbed Lucille and pinned her arms back. At that moment, Ramsay gave the word "Go" over his mic to his men, and they swarmed in.

Sheila stood there watching as Ryan handed her mother-in-law to the police. Alicia heard Sheila tell her as she was being led away, "You're right, Lucille. This ends now."

***

The van occupants let out a long breath. Gilly said, "Can I go to Billy now?"

"You certainly may," Stryder said. He wiped a hand across his brow. "I'm sure Anderson would've taken a bullet for Sheila, but let's be glad no blood was shed."

Ramsay walked to his wife. "I'll go with you to find Billy."

Alicia followed a distance behind the couple as Stryder went to check his men and the woman they had in their custody in back of one of the unmarked police cars.

Billy was with a tall officer by the park swings. As soon as he saw his mother, he jumped off the swing and ran to her. Gilly, tears running down her face, embraced her boy. "Billy, are you okay? Did she hurt you?"

Ramsay looked on, a bit uncertain as to his role in this dynamic. Alicia, behind him, felt the same.

"I'm okay, Mom. She was a strange lady. She kept calling me Tommy, but Mrs. Horse Lady and her kids were nice to me. They fed me McDonalds and lots of candy."

Gilly smiled through her tears. "I guess you heard Mrs. Kleisman's nickname. Although I never liked the woman, I think I owe her a thank you."

"Let's get you home, Son. It's cold out here." Ramsay blew out a puff of steam.

"Aren't you finishing up with your men?" Gilly asked.

"Not now. I want to bring my wife and boy home." He put an arm around her, and the three walked toward his car. They stopped suddenly and looked back at Alicia. Gilly said, "We'll drop you home. Thanks so much for coming. It meant a lot to me."

Alicia joined the three. She was glad she would have good news to tell John.

***

John was waiting for her at the door. He knew as soon as he saw her face that everything had turned out alright.

"It's over, John," she said. "Gilly and Ramsay have Billy back, and Sheila's mother-in-law has been arrested."

John sighed. "What a relief. I was worried. I'm glad no one was hurt."

Alicia followed John into the living room. "How are the twins?"

"Sleeping soundly."

She smiled. "I think I need a nightcap. I'm still keyed up."

"You also look cold. Come sit by the fire with me."

While she took a chair in one of the rockers by their fireplace, John brought two glasses of wine. "This'll warm you up and also this." He bent down and placed a quick kiss on her lips and then sat next to her. "You may not feel up to rehashing everything, and I'll understand if you don't, but if you'd like to talk about it, I wouldn't mind hearing how it all went down."

Alicia took a sip of the wine. "I thought you would, John. Sheila was very brave. Ryan went to help her, even though he wasn't supposed to be there. Lucille had taken the gun from Kleisman's house . . ."

"What?" John stopped her. "Alicia, I didn't know she'd be armed. My God, how did they get Billy away from her?"

"He broke free himself when she raised the gun at them."

John's gaze was intense. "That's amazing. How did they escape? Did the police rush in?"

"They couldn't. Ramsay was afraid it would set her off. Sheila tried talking to her. She mentioned her grandchildren. It seems one of Julie's daughters looks like her grandfather."

"Did that help?"

"No." Alicia took another swallow of wine. Reaction was starting to sink in and, despite the warmth of the fire, she began to shiver. "It was scary, John. We heard her release the safety. Luckily, it wasn't loaded. Kleisman was keeping it in her house for protection, but it looks like she didn't keep any bullets in it."

"Good for us. I wonder if they'll let her go now."

"I would think so. She warned us about Lucille." She paused. "If you don't mind, let's talk about something else. This has been a harrowing night."

John reached over and took her hand. "Sorry, Ali. I know it helps sometimes to talk things over, but you must be exhausted. Why don't we go to bed?"

Alicia got up and followed him upstairs. As she passed the twins' room, she looked in on them. She thought about Lucille Whitehead putting her only child to sleep and felt a pang of sympathy for her, but then she pushed it away. That type of love wasn't normal. It was obsessive and greedy.

As she joined John in bed, she took a quick glance at her cell phone that she placed in the charger on the side table. There was a text. It was from Sheila.

Alicia, I didn't want to call because of the hour. Thanks so much for all your help. I'm coming to work tomorrow and want to celebrate. We still owe Gilly and Ramsay a party, and I owe them my life. Please meet me a half hour before we open. I have all the decorations and gifts from last time locked up in the library supply cabinet. It'll be a surprise for everyone. I'll put a sign up for the public that we're opening an hour late as soon as Gilly arrives. We'll get Ramsay there, too.

"What is it?" John asked, seeing Alicia's face change as she read the message.

"Sheila wants to have that party for Gilly and Ramsay tomorrow. I think she also wants to celebrate finally being free of her mother-in-law's shadow."

John nodded. "I'd say that's fitting. I'll arrange for Dad to watch the twins, so I can be there with you, too."

Alicia was about to thank John for planning to join her at the library party when the front doorbell rang.

"Who could that be at this hour?" John asked.

"I'll get it," She donned her robe and slipped out of bed.

"I don't want you answering the door alone after all that's happened around here," John said, following her. As they passed the nursery, they noticed the twins were still sleeping soundly.

Because John was right behind her, Alicia didn't check the peephole before opening the door.

On their doorstep, shivering from the cold in a mini skirt and t-shirt, was Mrs. Kleisman's eldest daughter, Hilda.

Chapter Twenty-Eight

Tears ran down Hilda's face. "You're the library lady, aren't you? I thought this was your house. My Mom showed it to me once while we were walking."

"Yes, I'm Mrs. McKinney. You can call me Alicia. You're Hilda Kleisman, right?"

"That's me." The girl nodded, still shaking. "Come in. Get out of the cold." Alicia stepped back. John stood there silently observing the fifteen-year-old's entrance.

"John, why don't you get her a blanket? She looks like she's freezing. I'll make her some tea."

"Okay, but I'd like to know what she's doing here first." He looked at the girl warily. Hilda followed Alicia to the rocker by the fire.

"I wanted to run away," she said. "My mom called and told my sister she was coming home from prison. I disobeyed her and let the crazy woman and the boy go. Now I'm in trouble, and all because I took the money." She ended her story in sobs and collapsed onto the rocker.

Alicia nodded to John who disappeared upstairs to retrieve a blanket. "It's okay, Hilda. Your mother won't be mad. The police have Mrs. Burke, I mean Mrs. Whitehead in custody, and Billy's home with his family."

That didn't seem to appease her. "I also took the bullets out of the gun. I didn't want the lady to hurt anyone." She sniffled. "It's not that I'm afraid of being punished. I just hate living there. I feel sorry for my sisters. Mother doesn't care about anyone but herself. I thought the money the woman gave me would help me get away. I have a boyfriend, but his parents would never allow me to stay with him. I don't know where to go. Can you help, please?"

Alicia didn't have any experience with teenagers, but she sensed the girl needed someone to talk to. "Let me get you some tea to warm you up, and then we can chat. My husband is bringing you a blanket. Did you leave without a coat?"

"I don't have a coat. Mom refused to let me buy one. She says it's a frivolous expense, and I can get by with sweaters and layering my clothes."

While Alicia was pondering this comment, John arrived with a fluffy sky-blue blanket that she recognized as one they wrapped the twins in when they were cold. She couldn't imagine a parent denying a child warmth.

"Here you go," John said, handing Hilda the blanket. She bundled herself in it up to her chin. Her teeth were still chattering, but her tears had started to dry. "Thank you, Mr. McKinney."

"You can call me by my first name. It's John. Alicia, were you getting that tea? I'll have a cup too, but I'd like to bring it into the office. I need to write the story about tonight for the paper. I can't assign that to Andy. He's still on personal leave."

Alicia made the tea and brought the three cups out to them. Even though she knew John had to write the story, she also realized he was giving her time alone with Hilda.

"Are you going to call my mother?" the girl asked as she sipped her tea.

"I should let her know you're safe. You may think she doesn't care, but she's your mom."

"You're wrong. She's never told me she loves me. I don't think she wanted me or my sisters. Dad left her because he couldn't stand how she treated him. I wish he would've taken us."

Alicia's heart went out to the girl. She thought of Carol and how she hoped they'd form a close bond. She realized teenagers often broke away from their parents, but she knew this was more than that. She'd seen Mrs. Kleisman's house and how her kids were left alone to fend for themselves. She had reason to report her to child protection, but she wasn't sure that was the right thing to do.

"Hilda, you can stay here tonight, and I won't call your mom, but we need to make a decision tomorrow. You can sleep on the couch and use the bathroom on this floor if you want to wash up. I don't know if I have any clothes that can fit you, but I'll check my closet." She thought of the maternity clothes she still hadn't donated to charity. Hilda was a large girl, so they might be her size.

Alicia found a t-shirt and sweatpants that fit the girl, so she could remove her skimpy clothing. After she left her on the couch, she went to the office to tell John. He looked up from his computer. "I think you did the right thing, Ali, but she has to go back home tomorrow. If Kleisman finds out we kept her daughter, she could press charges. Hilda's a minor."

"I realize that, John, but it's nearly midnight. We'll bring her home in the morning."

"Okay." John hit a few keys on the keyboard and then closed the Word document he was writing. "I'll finish this tomorrow. I need to speak with Ramsay, anyway. C'mon, Alicia. Let's go to bed." He got up and walked with her upstairs.

After they'd tended to their nighttime rituals and slid into bed next to one another, Alicia said, "You know, John, this situation with Hilda and Sheila's mother-in-law makes me understand how hard it is to be a parent. I saw how much damage a mother or father can do to a child. Mrs. Whitehead was obsessive about her son, smothering him with what she considered love. Mrs. Kleisman is the opposite. She treats her kids like objects. There's got to be a healthy in between."

John sighed. "That's why there are so many therapists and psychiatrists." Alicia knew John had seen one for years but not because of any parental issues but because of his grief over the death of his wife.

"What if we talk with Mrs. Kleisman, maybe stage an intervention?"

"Ali, you can't help but try to involve yourself in emotional matters. I believe we'd be attempting a lost cause. Hilda will be old enough soon to break away."

"What about her sisters? Hilda's the oldest."

"They'll manage, honey. Things may not be as bad as they say. All kids think they have it tough especially the spoiled ones. Our kids are going to hate us in a few years."

"Please don't say that, John." Alicia didn't tell him what she and Gilly saw when they visited the Kleisman house, but she couldn't wipe away the memory.

"I went through a rebellious stage, too, when I went away to college. I was older, of course, but my parents were the last ones I wanted to listen to. I regret that now."

"Your dad still has a lot of wisdom to share," she said, thinking of Mac and his sharp witticisms.

"Yes, but Mom's gone. I hope Hilda and her sisters don't make the same mistake I made. Kleisman may not be June Cleaver, but she's their mother." He reached over and turned off the lamp on the bedside table. "It's late, and it's been a hard night. Let's get some sleep. We'll talk more in the morning."

***

As it turned out, they didn't get much of a chance to talk the next day. Since it was Monday, John prepared breakfast. He made sure to make enough for Hilda. The girl was delighted with the twins. She played peek-a-boo games with them and helped feed them. "I'm used to babysitting my sisters if you ever need help with Carol and Johnny," she offered.

Alicia thought that a great idea. Kim was finishing up her last year of college and busy with her plans for the future. Mac, as much as he loved his grandkids, wasn't getting any younger and neither was Betty.

Hilda seemed in bright spirits despite her tears and angry words against her mother the previous night, and Alicia wondered if John was right and that this was just a temperamental teen outburst.

"Is it okay if we call your mother now?" Alicia asked as Hilda was helping her clear the table. John was cleaning up the twins' high chair plates.

Hilda's face changed. "I thought you said I could stay."

"That was last night," Alicia explained. "You need to go home today. If you want, I'll bring you there. I have to get to the library early to help my boss set something up, but I can drop you on my way."

Hilda looked as if she was on the verge of tears again, but then she shrugged. "Okay. I'm not happy about going back, but I guess I have no choice. I actually miss my sisters already even though they can be pains sometimes." She smiled wanly.

John said, "I've found there are advantages to growing up as an only child. Ali and I don't have siblings, although I have a half-sister I found out about only a few years ago." He mentioned Pamela who was currently away on one of her European tours with her daughters. He turned to Alicia. "I have to finish my report today, but I'll meet you at the library in an hour or so for the party. I'll get Dad to come over and watch the twins while I'm there."

"Thanks, John," she said, giving him a goodbye kiss and then kissing each of the twins. While it used to be hard leaving them when she went to work, she'd adjusted to it and valued the time they had together.

She waited while Hilda got her things together. She had changed back into the clothes she'd worn the night before and used the downstairs bathroom to freshen up.

"I'm all set," the girl pronounced as she met Alicia by the door. Although there was still a shadow of sadness in her eyes, she seemed more accepting of being brought home to her mother.

John waved to them as they drove off. The twins stood next to him.

***

"What are you going to tell her?" Hilda asked as they turned down her block.

"You mean, your mom? We tell her the truth. You were upset and came to my house. I let you stay the night because it was very late, too late to call. Don't worry. She'll understand."

"You don't know my mom. She'll understand, alright, but she won't care. That's the problem."

Alicia's heart went out to the girl. She again wished there was something she could do.

Parking in the street by the house, Alicia checked her watch and asked Hilda, "What time do you have to be in school?"

"My first class at the high school is eight fifteen."

"You'll have to hurry, but I think you'll make it. I don't have to meet my friend at the library until eight. Let me go in and speak to your mother first. Just wait here, please."

Hilda lowered her head.

"You're not going to run again, are you?" Alicia knew she risked Hilda making a dash for it, but she wanted to talk with Mrs. Kleisman alone.

"No. I promise. I did a stupid thing. I didn't think about the consequences." Her eyes started to fill again.

"It's going to be okay, Hilda. We go through bad spells in life, but things have a way of working out. Your mom may seem indifferent, but I'm sure deep down she cares about you."

A nod was the extent of Hilda's reply.

Alicia got out and walked to the door. Her knock was answered by one of Hilda's sisters. "You're that lady who was here the other night. What do you want?"

"Is your mother here?"

"You're not taking her back to the cops, are you?"

"No. I need to talk to her. Can you please get her?"

"She's busy." Alicia knew the girl was lying. "I'm Alicia McKinney. I don't know your name, but I'm here about your sister Hilda."

The girl regarded her with large dark eyes. "Hilda's not here. She ran away. I'm mad at her because she didn't take me with her."

Alicia didn't know how to reply to this, but she was saved the trouble by Mrs. Kleisman who came up behind her daughter. "What's going on? Who's that at the door?" She stopped as she recognized Alicia. "Oh, Mrs. Ramsay's friend. Did the sheriff send you with my reward? I knew he'd come up with something after how I led him to the killer."

"Mrs. Kleisman, I'm not here with money. I need to speak with you about your daughter, Hilda." She glanced at the other girl and added, "Alone."

She was afraid Mrs. Kleisman would shut the door in her face, but the woman stepped back. "Come in." She turned to her daughter. "Get ready for school, Hannah, and make sure Haley is ready, too."

As Hannah walked away, Alicia entered the house. It was in the same condition as she and Gilly had previously found it with food wrappers and clothes scattered everywhere. Kleisman didn't seem to be embarrassed by the mess. Without offering Alicia coffee or anything else, she said, "What about Hilda? I didn't know she was missing until this morning. I was home late last night, and Hannah said something to me, but I was too tired to listen."

"I'm afraid your daughter ran away," Alicia said, "She came to my house, and I let her stay the night. She's in my car now, but I wanted to speak to you about some things she told me. She's unhappy and thinks you don't care about her."

Mrs. Kleisman directed her beady eyes on Alicia. "I don't know where she gets that idea. I love all my children. After my ex left, I did my best to raise them. It isn't easy. The alimony I get doesn't cover much, and it's always late. I can't find work anywhere. It seems no one wants to hire a fat, middle aged woman who never graduated high school."

Alicia realized Kleisman, behind her double chins, was younger than she appeared, younger than herself. She must've had her children early in life. "I know it must've been difficult for you, but Hilda is at a tough age, and your younger girls are growing up, too. They need to know they're important to you."

Kleisman's eyes suddenly began to tear up. She wiped at them. "I love my kids, Mrs. McKinney. Maybe I've been too worried about paying the bills and keeping this house. Maybe I need to keep looking for work no matter what job is open. Maybe I need to go on a good diet and feel better about myself, so I can be an example to my daughters."

Alicia thought about what she'd told Hilda about how bad situations could turn around, just as her life did after Peter died. "Mrs. Kleisman, I may have an offer for you, but let me get Hilda in, so she can get ready for school. I have to be at work myself, but I'll be back to you soon about my idea."

"Thank you, Mrs. McKinney."

When Alicia brought Hilda in, Mrs. Kleisman wrapped the girl in a big hug. "I'm sorry, Hild, for how I've been acting toward you. I'm going to try to change."

"Mother," Hilda said. "I'm sorry I didn't listen to you and let that lady and boy leave, but she gave me fifty dollars." She took off her backpack and reached in the front. "You can have the money."

"No," Mrs. Kleisman said. "Keep it, Hilda. Buy yourself something nice. I'm getting myself a job. Mrs. McKinney says she knows a place that might take me."

Hilda turned to Alicia. "That's wonderful. Thank you so much for letting me stay at your house last night and for helping my mother find work. If you need a babysitter for your cute kids, remember that I'm available."

Alicia gave her a hug. "I'll certainly call you if we need you." As she left, Alicia looked back at mother and daughter standing together and thought that John was wrong after all. There really was always something that you can do if you got involved.

Feeling happy, she put her key in the ignition and was about to drive off when she heard a noise behind her and felt a metal object against her neck.

"Don't move. This one has bullets."

Chapter Twenty-Nine

Her heart began to race. "Mrs. Whitehead. You were in jail."

"Not for long. That officer Ramsay left to watch me let me out when I asked to use the restroom. He didn't count on my kicking him in the groin and making my escape while he rolled around on the floor in pain."

John had told Alicia that they were planning to transport Lucille to the state jail today but that she would spend the night in the sheriff's one-cell office. "They'll find you missing. Police will be all over Cobble Cove."

"Not before I finish my mission to avenge my son. Now drive away a little bit, so we can talk more freely."

When Alicia hesitated, Lucille pressed the gun deeper into her neck. "Do it, or you'll never see your handsome husband or twins again."

Alicia obeyed, driving a few blocks until Lucille told her to pull over into a wooded area. "Much better. Now here's the plan, Alicia. You need to call Sheila and arrange to meet her. Is she working at the library today?"

Alicia knew Sheila was already at the library preparing for Gilly's party. She tried to think of a story to make up to fool Lucille, but she wasn't a convincing liar. "Yes," she replied, her voice tight.

"Good. We'll meet her in the parking lot. You tell her to come to your car. You need help bringing in some heavy books or something. No, wait, she might ask one of the men to do that. Think of something else. Just make sure you get her to come alone."

Alicia knew Sheila was sharp and would be able to see through whatever story she offered. "Okay, but maybe I should go in to ask her."

"I'm not stupid. You call from the car and then I take your phone. One slip up, and goodbye family." She pressed the gun into Alicia's neck hard enough to make her wince.

She knew there was no sense reasoning with the woman, so Alicia decided to play along. "If I do this, will you let me go?"

"Yes. It's Sheila I want. She caused me years of pain by killing my boy."

"What if they catch you? You'll be back in a cell for life."

Lucille laughed. "Ha. How much life do you think I have left? My life ended the day she married Tommy."

When Alicia didn't respond, Lucille said, "What are you waiting for? Drive to the library and then make that call."

***

Since it was an hour before opening time, the library parking lot was deserted except for Sheila's car. Alicia wished Sheila had asked Nancy to come decorate for the party instead of her. At least then there would be another person in the building. However, she also knew that Gladys, the custodian, would arrive in a half hour. There was no way she could keep Lucille talking until then.

As soon as they were parked, Lucille said, "Go on. I see she's here. Make that call."

Alicia took her phone from her coat pocket. Her mind was racing with what to say to warn Sheila. As she was about to dial, another call was coming through. She saw it was John on the display.

"My husband's calling. Should I not accept?"

"No. Answer it. You don't want him to suspect anything. Be calm and act like everything is okay. Put it on speaker, so I can hear."

Alicia accepted the call and pressed the speaker button. "Hi, John. What's up?"

"Ali, how did things go with Hilda?"

"Good. She's home with her mother. Are the twins okay?"

Lucille pressed the gun into her neck again and whispered, "Keep it short."

"They're fine," John said, "Dad will be here in a few minutes. What time should I be at the library?"

"Uh, in an hour. Sheila and I have to set up first."

"Great! See you then. Love ya." He sent a kiss through the phone.

"Love you, too, my darling."

"Hang up and call now," Lucille said in the same low voice.

Alicia still hadn't thought how to warn Sheila. She just hoped John would understand the secret message she'd sent him. She'd signed off with "my darling," the phrase she and John had chosen as code words if they were ever in a situation where they needed help but couldn't talk freely. The phone was still on speaker, so Lucille could hear everything she said.

"I'm dialing her cell because she won't answer the library phone until we open."

Lucille didn't comment but stuck the gun's barrel deeper into Alicia's neck. The phone rang a few times. Alicia's heart beat on each ring.

Chapter Thirty

Lucille grabbed the phone and disconnected the call. "What are you doing?" Alicia exclaimed.

"I've got a better idea. I'm taking you in. Get out of the car, slowly." Alicia obeyed. Although she thought she might be able to outrun the woman, she doubted she could dodge a bullet.

Lucille came up behind her and stuck the gun in her back. "Take me through the employee's entrance," she commanded.

At the back door, Alicia fumbled with the keypad. "I may have forgotten the code."

"Don't play with me." Lucille pushed the gun into her spine. "If you don't open the door, I'll shoot it open, but I'll shoot you first."

Alicia complied, feeling her stomach drop. There had to be a way to disarm Lucille. She wished she'd taken self-defense and could use some karate moves on her.

"Now be quiet and walk slowly."

Alicia took small steps down the hall. She wondered if Lucille realized that Sheila was upstairs in the break room and not at the front desk. She decided to keep her downstairs as long as possible.

The lights were dim in this part of the library since Gladys hadn't arrived yet and Sheila hadn't turned all the switches up. As they approached the main part of the library, Alicia considered running into the stacks to hide, but she couldn't risk Lucille shooting her before she got there.

"Where is she?" Lucille asked, looking around the empty room.

Alicia felt the gun at her back. "She's upstairs."

"Is there an elevator?"

Alicia glanced over her shoulder. "Over there."

Lucille pushed her forward. "Let's take it up. I don't want Sheila hearing two sets of footsteps on the stairs."

They rode up in silence. Alicia's heart was still hammering in her chest. Even if John had understood the secret code word they'd created after she and Gilly had been confronted by a killer in a hotel nearly a year ago and alerted Ramsay, chances were they wouldn't get to the library in time.

As they stepped off the elevator, Alicia heard Sheila humming from the staff room. She hummed when she was happy, and it broke Alicia's heart knowing that the safety she thought she now had was an illusion.

"Keep walking. I want to surprise her. I'm sure she'll be thrilled to see her mother-in-law again." The sarcasm dripped from her words. Alicia had a fleeting thought of yelling a warning to Sheila, but her boss and friend wouldn't be able to escape the confines of the staff room which only had one exit unless you counted the window.

They were only a few steps from the door. Lucille whispered instructions. "Go ahead in. Act normal. I'll be waiting at the door to make my entrance. Remember, I won't mind shooting both of you if you do anything reckless." She stuck the gun hard into Alicia's back for emphasis and then pushed her forward.

"Alicia. You're here. Good. I thought I heard the elevator come up." Sheila was holding some balloons. "I need these blown up." She glanced at the clock on the wall that read 9:15. "We don't have much time."

Alicia winced at the irony of her remark. She took the balloons she was handed. The room looked beautiful. A long table had been brought out and set with paper goods in pastel colors—pink, white, and lavender. The two red hearts with Gilly and Ron's names were hung from the ceiling. The unopened gifts sat on a smaller table.

"Ryan and Julie are bringing the food," she said. "They should be here in a few minutes. I didn't want it to get cold, so I told them to wait until nine forty-five. Gilly and Ramsay are coming at ten. I already put up a sign outside and a message on the answering machine that we're opening late this morning."

"You've thought of everything, Sheila," Lucille said, stepping into the room.

Sheila gasped. "Lucille! What are you doing here?"

"Surprising you. It's a surprise party you're setting up, isn't it?"

"You were in jail. How did you . . ."

"I'm not here to talk. I'm here to finish a job." She walked forward, pointing the gun at Sheila.

"Put that down," Sheila said. Alicia could see the fear in her eyes. "Killing me won't bring back Tom. All it will do is send you to jail for life."

"I already told her"—she glanced at Alicia—"that I have no life left. You took the only thing away that meant anything to me."

"I didn't kill Tom," Sheila said in a firm voice that broke slightly. "I loved him. Can't you understand that?"

Alicia knew Lucille was beyond understanding, but they had to keep her talking until someone arrived to help.

"Love. You know nothing about love," Lucille said, walking further into the room. "You're with that professor now. Shows you how much you cared for my son."

"I honored Tom's memory for thirty years. I've finally found someone who I care about again, but that doesn't mean he's replacing Tom. No one can do that."

"You're right about that. I've waited all these years to see that his death is brought to justice. No more stalling. You pay now." She raised the gun higher and began to pull back the trigger. Alicia held her breath as Sheila jumped away and the bullet whizzed past her into the wall of the storage room that also served as Sneaky's cat room.

"You have nowhere to run, so stop dodging." Lucille raised the gun again; but, just as she did so, Alicia caught sight of Sneaky who'd crawled through his cat flap after hearing the noise from the connecting room. A sound that she'd never heard Sneaky make, a cross between a yowl and a growl, issued from his mouth as, claws extended, he launched himself at Lucille's leg. She screamed in pain as the cat's sharp nails gripped her calf, and she was thrown off balance. Alicia, seeing her chance, rushed forward and grabbed the gun as it fell from her grip.

"Looks like you and cats don't mix," Alicia said. She stood over Lucille who'd fallen to the floor. Sneaky came to her side. She bent down and petted him. "Thanks, Sneak. Good job!"

Sheila looked on in shock as the elevator dinged. Ramsay and John rushed into the room. John's anxious expression was replaced by a brief smile as he saw Alicia standing over Lucille, Sheila safely at her side. Ramsay strode over to Lucille, pulled her to her feet, and locked her hands behind her. Taking handcuffs from his pocket he cuffed her and said, "You won't escape this time. I'm taking you personally to the state jail this morning." He then read her the Miranda rights.

Accepting defeat, Whitehead glared at him.

Sheila walked over to her. "You had everything wrong, Lucille. Your twisted idea of love for your son and your belief that I harmed him. I don't know if you're insane or evil, but I'm sorry it had to end this way. I loved Tom in a real and special way, and what you've done hasn't tarnished my memory or removed him from my heart. I want you to know that."

Lucille lowered her head and issued no word of reply as Ramsay led her away, taking the gun Alicia handed him as he left.

Chapter Thirty-One

After Ramsay took Lucille away, John hugged Alicia. "Smart going using our code words," he said. "I almost thought it was a false alarm."

"I was afraid you wouldn't understand because we rarely use them, but they're ones that wouldn't tip off Lucille."

"I won't ask what your code phrase is," Sheila said, "but I'm thankful you have one and that we took in this little guy." She picked up Sneaky.

"It's odd that Sneaky and KittyKai both foiled your mother-in-law," Alicia said. "I guess I missed something." John's smile widened as he watched Sheila petting the Siamese. Alicia knew she'd grown fond of him, even though it had taken a few years. She still left his feeding and litter box cleaning to Laura after Mac retired from the job.

"We're going to need to patch that hole," Sheila said, looking at the gap above the cat door. "At least it isn't in the public space."

"What about the party?" Alicia asked. "People will be arriving in a few minutes." Just as she said that, Ryan and Julie walked through the door carrying the food. They'd been so absorbed that they hadn't heard the elevator let them off.

"I'd say you have even more of a reason to celebrate now," John said. "Unfortunately, Ramsay will be delayed."

Ryan, placing a bag of bagels and cream cheese spread on the table, said, "What happened? What are you all talking about?"

Julie, more observant than Sheila's boyfriend, walked toward the hole in the back wall. "Oh my God! Is that a bullet hole?"

Sheila nodded. "Afraid so. Your grandmother was back, but thanks to our library cat and Alicia, she's in jail for good."

Julie hugged Sheila. "Oh, Mom. I should've been here."

"No. I'm glad you weren't put in danger." Ryan said, "I'm sorry you had to go through that, Sheila. I'm sure it brought back some very painful memories."

Sheila broke free of Julie's embrace, clasped her hand and led her to Ryan. She put her arms around the two of them. "Although there was no love lost between me and Lucille, she brought me Tom who gave me you, Julie." She turned to Ryan. "And now I have you, Ryan."

Alicia felt awkward around this family tableau. She went to John and asked him to help her put out the breakfast food and baked goods Julie and Ryan had brought. As they worked, Sneaky looked up with blue pleading eyes, and she dropped a few crumbs his way on purpose.

***

There were still a few minutes until people would arrive. Sheila approached Alicia. "There's one more thing we should do before the party. Come to my office. I have some paintings in there. I'd like you to help me choose one to cover the bullet hole. There's no reason people need to know what happened right away. I don't want to spoil the party."

Alicia followed her down the hall. When they were inside the room, Sheila closed the door. "Alicia, I only have one painting that will work on that wall, but the reason I asked you to come with me is because I had to speak with you about something. That's also the reason I wanted you to help me set up the party. I would've asked Nancy, but I thought we'd have some time alone."

Alicia was puzzled. "What did you want to tell me? Have I done anything wrong?"

Sheila smiled. "Not at all. Have a seat. This won't take long. We don't have much time."

Alicia sat in the chair by Sheila's desk while her boss remained standing by it. "I've made a decision that I've put off for too long. You recall that I've wanted to retire and move to California to be near Julie and her family, right?"

Alicia nodded. Her heart started to beat fast. "Are you leaving the library?"

Sheila directed her emerald gaze at her and said, "Yes, but not right away." She waved her hands full of rings. "I need to put someone in place that I can trust. The Board will need to make the final decision, but I have a recommendation. You."

"Me? You want me to take over as director?"

"If you will accept the offer and the Board approves which I think they will. I'm making the announcement at the party today, but I'm not mentioning you. I know you need some time to think this over and discuss it with John."

"Sheila, I'm honored, but you know I have young children."

"They'll be in pre-school by the time I go." Sheila walked to her wall to a framed photo of Cobble Cove. Alicia recognized it as the view from Cove Point, the town's mountain atop which she and John had once had a picnic in November and gotten to know one another when she first came there. Sheila lifted it off its hook. "We'll use this to cover the hole in the wall. Let's get back and take care of it."

"What if I decide not to take your offer? Do you have anyone else in mind?" Alicia's mind was spinning with the pluses and minuses of becoming a library director.

"No. You've been here the longest and had many years of library experience from when you lived on Long Island. I also trust you the most, but once the position is announced, they'll interview other librarians who apply for the job. However, this isn't a Civil Service library, so we're not restricted to hiring off a list."

"Okay," Alicia said. "I'll think about it. Thank you for considering me."

Sheila did a very un-Sheila-like thing. Putting the painting on her desk, she came to Alicia and hugged her. "I'm going to miss you so much, Alicia, but I think I can build a life with Ryan. I feel like I'm finally free from my past and can make a new start. You, of all people, should understand that."

"Yes," Alicia said, recalling how she'd traveled to Cobble Cove and found John after the death of her husband. "I do, and I wish you all the best."

Sheila stepped back, wiping a tear from the corner of her eye. "Mac used to say, 'things happen for a reason.' This experience with Lucille has taught me that he was right. Now, let's go hang a painting."

***

Only a few minutes after they returned and Alicia had helped Sheila hang the Cove Point painting over the bullet hole, people began to arrive. Nancy was first, carrying a tray of pastries. Alicia figured she must've stopped at Claire's bakery on the way. Donald showed up next empty handed but with a smile as he noticed the food on the table. "Glad I waited for breakfast. Roger made those whole wheat vegetable pancakes again." He made a face. Alicia knew how he felt about his partner's healthy food recipes.

When Laura got there, she noticed Sneaky under the table. Alicia thought he was avoiding his room because of the bullet that had entered it, but it was more likely he was waiting for more scraps. Laura said, "Hey, Sneaks, you're joining us for the party." She looked toward Sheila who usually kept strict rules about Sneaky entering the staff room, although it was common knowledge he visited frequently.

Sheila said, "I'm making an exception today, but don't give him too many table scraps or we'll be taking him to the vet."

The rest of the staff were all there by the time Gilly and Ramsay were expected. Sheila turned off the lights and told everyone to be quiet so that when the guests of honor arrived, they could surprise them. Alicia wasn't sure Ramsay would be back yet, although the state jail wasn't that far a trip. She wondered if there would be a lot of paperwork and other details involved in Lucille's arrest that would hold up his return. Her concerns were erased when he walked through the door with Gilly.

"Surprise!" they all shouted.

Although Ramsay was in on the party, having been there earlier and told not to mention anything to his wife, Gilly seemed genuinely surprised. "What's going on?" she asked, looking around in bewilderment, her dark eyes widening as she took in the heart-shaped balloons, the banner with her and Ramsay's name on it, and the wrapped gifts on the table.

"Since you ran off with the sheriff and we didn't get a chance to celebrate your wedding, we thought we'd have a party for you two," Sheila explained.

"How sweet. Thank you." When she caught sight of Sneaky who'd peeked his head from under the tablecloth, she laughed. "I guess Sneaky wanted to be included. Too bad I didn't bring KittyKai."

Laura said, "We're having a story time for the children in a few weeks. KittyKai is invited as Sneaky's guest." She glanced toward Sheila who nodded and said, "What an excellent idea, Laura."

***

When the party was over, everyone was told what had happened earlier that morning. Sheila included the information following her announcement of her retirement and move to California. It sounded like good and bad news to Alicia. Nothing was mentioned about Sheila's replacement, but Alicia saw John's eyebrow quirk in her direction when Sheila said that the Board would be interviewing candidates for the director's position in the next few months.

The information about Whitehead was met with relief and audible sighs. Donald said, "I knew that Madame Defarge wasn't to be trusted."

"How did you get her to the state jail so fast?" Alicia inquired.

Ramsay, chewing on a bagel, swallowed, and replied, "I may have exceeded the highway speed limit, but I couldn't wait to get that woman out of Cobble Cove."

Ryan put an arm over Sheila. "We're thankful to you for all you did."

Sheila said, "Although my decision to retire has been long in the making, I'll miss you all. I hope that some of you will come visit me in California, and I'll try to take a few trips back to check up on things here."

"I'd love to go to California," Gilly said. She glanced at Ramsay. "Maybe an anniversary trip?"

"It would be great for us, too," John put in. "Ali keeps telling me we should take a vacation from Cobble Cove now that the kids are getting older."

"Then it's settled," Sheila said. "but don't pack your bags too soon. I'm not leaving just yet. I want some time to train my new successor." Her emerald gaze landed on Alicia, who felt other eyes upon her in speculation.

***

That night, in bed after the kids were tucked in, John turned to Alicia and said, "Sheila asked you to take her job, didn't she?"

Alicia smiled. "I knew you'd figure it out. Yes, she spoke to me about it when we went to get the painting in her office. She said to discuss it with you before I made a decision, but they still have to interview other people."

John shrugged. "Just a formality. It's yours if you want it, Ali."

She looked into his deep, blue eyes. "Are you sure? It'll mean more time away from you and the kids and less time for me to co-write our books."

He continued gazing at her. "Do you remember when I was interested in that job at Columbia, and you were upset because I would have to stay in the city during the week?"

The memory of their argument at that time caused Alicia to feel guilt creep through her. "I do, and I'm sorry. That would've been a great opportunity for you."

He shook his head. "No. It wouldn't have been. I've gained so much more being here with you, Carol, and Johnny. Our books are doing well. We're not raking in tons of dough from them, but people are starting to recognize us as authors. This position you're being offered is different. You've been a librarian for more than half your life. You won't be away from us, and you'll have the help of your staff to run the library. Sheila never had an assistant director, but maybe you want to appoint one. Donald is young. He might be interested, or maybe there'll be another applicant. I could post an announcement in the *Courier* if the Board approves it."

"Thanks, John. I'm glad you're supporting me on this, but I have to consider everything. Sheila says she won't be leaving immediately and that, by the time she does, the kids will be in pre-school. That's not too far away, but they'll still be young. I want to make sure I'm doing the right thing by them and by you."

John smiled and pulled her close to him. "Honey, we never know we're doing the right thing until we do it."

Alicia knew he was right. When she'd traveled to Cobble Cove in search of answers about her first husband's past, she had plenty of misgivings, but look where that had led her. She snuggled into John's arms and found her answer.

Chapter Thirty-Two

During the weeks following Lucille's capture and arrest, Alicia hadn't had much contact with Sheila who was away from the library attending meetings or behind closed doors in her office working on what Alicia imagined were her retirement plans. Because of this, Alicia hadn't had a chance to speak with her to give her an answer about her offer.

On the day scheduled for Sneaky story time, Alicia helped Laura gather the books for the children. Although Sneaky had been lying in his usual spot on the window seat of the Children's Room, Laura had placed him inside his cat carrier and moved him next to the chair in which she read the stories. She knew from experience that the noise level of the kids would disturb Sneaky, so she kept him in his box until the end of the program when she let each child have a turn at petting him. It was at that point, that she'd asked Gilly to bring KittyKai as Sneaky's special guest. That honor had only been bestowed upon Fido on special occasions.

"I think some cat books would be appropriate today," Alicia suggested as she helped Laura look through the waist high stacks of picture books that appealed to children up to five years old. The only older child they were allowing to the program that day was Angelina, who was especially fond of Sneaky and who'd recently had a successful bone marrow transplant for her leukemia. Because of the high chance of infection after the procedure, she hadn't been to school in several months but was now permitted to go out for short periods at a time. Her family was hoping she could resume classes in the spring.

"Great idea," Laura said pulling out a Cat in the Hat Dr. Seuss book and a collection of nursery rhymes that included *Three Blind Mice*, a nice choice for interactive finger play.

They'd just finished setting up when the sound of young, excited voices echoed through the room as parents holding the hands of their children led them to the tiny seats set up in the circle around Laura's chair.

"Good morning, Miss Carson. Mrs. McKinney," the children chanted. When they saw the carrier, they exclaimed, "Sneaky! Sneaky's here."

"Please have a seat, everyone," Laura said. "We'll be starting Sneaky Storytime in a few minutes. Today, Sneaky will have a special guest."

Her announcement was met with shrieks and whoops. A few mothers held their kids back from attacking the cat's carrier.

Laura calmly repeated the instructions, "Sit down, and we'll start. Afterward, you'll all get a chance to see Sneaky and his guest."

Alicia moved to the back of the circle and stood among the parents. John was late bringing Carol and Johnny, but he was also bringing Angelina. He arrived just as Laura picked up the first book from the pile on the table next to her. Alicia helped the twins settle into the two empty chairs in front of her. Angelina sat next to Carol in the one on the end of that aisle. Alicia hadn't seen the girl in a while and found it remarkable how healthy she looked. Although she was bundled up in a heavy coat, her pink cheeks seemed the result of her recovery and not of the cold because the February day was unseasonably warm. "Nice to see you, Angelina," Alicia whispered. "You look great."

"Thank you, Mrs. Mac," she said, calling Alicia by the nickname she'd coined for her. "I feel good."

Alicia couldn't say much more because Laura had started reading. She stepped back next to John. "Gilly is bringing KittyKai today," she told him. "I hope he and Sneaky don't get into another battle."

"I think they've ironed out their differences." John grinned. "Sometimes I think animals are better at that than people." She wondered if he was thinking of Lucille Whitehead. Ramsay had told them that her trial date was set but that she was being held in the state jail without bail until then.

***

Gilly somehow managed to arrive as the story time wound down. She carried KittyKai in her carrier and waited until Laura gave her the signal to come up front. Laura placed the final book down and said, "Alright, children, it's time for Sneaky and his special guest, KittyKai, to greet you all. Remember the rules—you get into a line, very quietly. One at a time, you may come up to pet both cats. Before you do that,"—she turned to Gilly who had placed KittyKai's box next to Sneaky's—"this is Mrs. Ramsay. She has brought her kitten, KittyKai, to join us today. Mrs. Ramsay, please take KittyKai out of her carrier."

Gilly opened the box and gently pulled out KittyKai. There was a loud murmur of oohs and aahs as the kids saw her.

"Does anyone know what type of cat KittyKai is?" Laura asked.

Angelina raised her hand. Laura nodded for her to answer. "She's a calico."

"Very good, Angelina. Calicos have three colors, black, orange, and white. They're almost always girl cats."

One of the kids, a young boy, asked, "Why?"

Laura replied, "I'll have Dr. Donna visit one day and explain that." Alicia knew that Dr. Donna Clark, the town vet, frequently came to story times to talk about pets and answer questions from the children.

"We don't have much more time," Laura said, "Form a line and come up quietly while I get Sneaky." Now was the moment Alicia dreaded even though John was convinced KittyKai and Sneaky were on good terms.

It was harder to remove Sneaky from his carrier than it had been to take out KittyKai, but he came as Laura expertly dragged him out. As a volunteer at a shelter, Laura knew all the tricks for dealing with felines. Once out, Sneaky eyed KittyKai whom Gilly was still holding in her arms. He didn't hiss or even meow. Alicia took that as his acceptance of KittyKai's presence.

Laura placed Sneaky on her lap and sat back down in her chair. Gilly remained standing with the kitten. The children came up as instructed and each spent a short time petting each cat. A few parents took photos. Carol and Johnny went up together, and Alicia used her phone to snap shots of them with Sneaky and KittyKai. Angelina was last. Alicia took some photos of her that she would send to Patty, the girl's mother, who was currently teaching at the public school.

The children reluctantly left with their parents, waving little hands at the cats. "Bye Sneaky," "Bye Kit Ki."

Alicia gave Carol and Johnny kisses as John took their hands. Angelina followed behind. "Have a good day, Ali," he said pecking her cheek. "I'll drop Angelina home and then maybe take the twins out somewhere. It's a nice day for February." He glanced out the sunlit windows.

Alicia knew that Gary, Angelina's dad, had started working half days for Duncan at the grocery store so he could be around to care for his daughter during her recovery. They'd also hired a morning nurse to be there after Patty left for work. She hoped that when Angelina was back at school, Gary could find a position that paid better for his family.

"Daddy, Sigh Moozeum?" Johnny asked.

"Maybe. Would you like that, too, Carol?"

Carol nodded enthusiastically, swinging the blonde braids Alicia had fashioned for her that morning.

"I used to love the science museum back home when I was younger," Angelina said.

Alicia felt bad that John couldn't extend the invitation to the girl, but she knew being out in the public for too long was against her doctor's orders until she was cleared in the spring.

She watched the four leave and then helped Laura put away the story time books. Gilly came over and placed KittyKai in her carrier. "I think that went rather well," she said.

"Thank you, Gilly," Laura said. "The kids always love to interact with Sneaky, and KittyKai was an added bonus today." Instead of putting Sneaky back in his box, she carried him to the window seat and watched him plop himself down in a sunny spot.

"I'll bring KittyKai back to the inn and then check in for work," Gilly said.

"See you later," Alicia told her friend as she returned to the Reference desk.

***

"Before you sit down, Sheila wants to see you," Donald said when Alicia joined him at Reference.

She had a feeling she knew what the director wanted. Heading upstairs, she took some deep breaths. Sheila's door was open. She sat behind her desk looking over some papers.

"May I come in?" Alicia asked.

"Yes, please, and close the door behind you."

Alicia followed her directions and took a seat when Sheila waved her toward the one by her desk.

"I think you know why I want to speak to you, Alicia," she said, adjusting the reading glasses she'd recently begun to wear.

"I do. You want my decision on whether I'd be interested in the director position."

"Correct." She glanced down at her desk and then back at Alicia. "We've already had several applicants. I need to know if you're interested in applying. I think you've had enough time to consider my offer and speak with John about it."

"Yes, I have." Alicia met her gaze. "I had some misgivings at first—the kids, John and my books, my qualifications for the job—but I believe this will be an opportunity for me. The first time I stepped through the library doors and John introduced me to Mac and Sneaky"— she laughed at the memory— "and then you . . . I felt like this place would play a special role in my life. I've come to know the patrons, many of whom have become friends. The improvements you and the Board made since I was hired have been wonderful, and the new staff members are dedicated and professional." She thought of Nancy, Laura, and Donald. "I've enjoyed working with them and have some ideas that I'd like to see implemented in the future to make the library even more of a learning and community center for the people of Cobble Cove."

Sheila smiled. "That's quite a speech. You have my vote, Alicia, if your answer is a 'yes,' that is."

"Yes, my answer is 'yes.' I'd be honored to take your place, Sheila, and I wish you all the best in California with Ryan, Julie, and your granddaughters."

Sheila stood up and walked around her desk. "I sometimes have a hard time showing my emotions, but that doesn't mean I don't feel deeply. You know that when I lost Tom, John was the friend who helped me deal with my sorrow. That's why I was thrilled when you two got together. You've been a friend as well as an employee, and I think you'll make a great director."

Alicia, thinking she was being dismissed, got up from her seat. Instead, Sheila embraced her. "I've had difficulty coming to terms with leaving Cobble Cove and the library, but now I feel relieved because I know I leave them in good hands. Thank you, Alicia."

They stood there a few minutes hugging and then Alicia broke away. "I guess I should get back to work," she said. Sheila shook her head. "One more thing. I'm not leaving just yet. Once a decision is made by the Board, I intend to train my successor." She went back to her desk, took a sheet of paper from it, and handed it to Alicia. "This is your application. Good luck."

Epilogue

It was the first day of spring in Cobble Cove and the initial meeting of the Library Cruisers Walking group. Because of all that had happened in February, the group's start had been postponed until a chilly March morning. Gilly, who'd first come up with the idea, gathered with everyone on the inn's steps. Nancy, in her smart zipped-up blue jogging suit, was already doing warm up stretches. Donald, wearing a tie sprinkled with tiny people lifting weights and cycling, was yawning as he checked his cell phone. Sheila looked wide awake as she adjusted the bright yellow headband that constrained her red locks. Alicia didn't know how she'd manage the two-mile route to the library in her high-heeled boots. Alicia had chosen comfortable sneakers and wore a puffy vest over sweatpants. She hoped the morning exercise would help her lose the pounds she'd added during the winter.

Gilly started a headcount. She held a sheet in front of her with the names of the employees and patrons who had signed up. She'd recently decided to open it to the public, and Sheila had agreed it was a good idea, even though only one patron had signed up so far but had brought her whole family. Rhonda Kleisman and her daughters Hilda, Hannah, and Haley stood among the group in their new matching jackets, ones she'd purchased at Chloe's Closet with an employee's discount. Smiling next to Alicia, she said, "I love my job. I can't thank you enough for introducing me to Chloe. She's put me in charge of her new line of plus-sized clothing."

As Gilly checked off the names of the participants and pulled the cord of the whistle she wore around her neck, Alicia said, "I'm glad you like working at Chloe's, but if you keep up with this group, you may not need to shop in the plus size department."

Mrs. Kleisman grinned.

Gilly blew the whistle, and they were off.

About Debbie De Louise

Debbie De Louise is an award-winning author and a reference librarian at a public library on Long Island. She is a member of Sisters-in-Crime, International Thriller Writers, and the Cat Writer's Association. She has a BA in English and an MLS in Library Science from Long Island University. Her novels include the five books of the Cobble Cove mystery series: A Stone's Throw, Between a Rock and a Hard Place, Written in Stone, Love on The Rocks, and No Gravestone Unturned. Debbie has also written a standalone mystery, Reason to Die, a romantic comedy novella, When Jack Trumps Ace, and a paranormal romance, Cloudy Rainbow. She lives on Long Island with her husband, Anthony; daughter, Holly; and cat Stripey.

Social Media:

Facebook:
https://www.facebook.com/debbie.delouise.author/

Twitter: https://twitter.com/Deblibrarian

Goodreads:

https://www.goodreads.com/author/show/2750133

Amazon Author Page: http://amzn.to/2bIHdaQ
Website/Blog/Newsletter Sign Up:

https://debbiedelouise.com

Acknowledgements:

I'd like to thank the fine staff at Solstice Publishing especially Kathi Sprayberry, Melissa Miller, and Kate Collins for all their hard work on behalf of their authors. They are truly an amazing publisher, and I'm very lucky to be part of this group. I would also like to acknowledge my fellow Solstice authors and other author friends as well as my family and all those who have supported me on my publishing journey. A special thanks to Florence Evans who won my newsletter's cat-naming contest with the name of her own cat, a pretty calico named Kittykai. Last but not least, I give my heartfelt thanks to my readers for their interest and encouragement in the Cobble Cove mystery series. I love writing for all of you. Thanks for reading.

If you enjoyed this story, check out these other Solstice Publishing books by Debbie De Louise:

The Cobble Cove Mysteries: A Stone's Throw, Between a Rock and a Hard Place, Written in Stone, Love on the Rocks, and No Gravestone Unturned.

Follow Alicia the librarian's journey to the small town of Cobble Cove, New York after her husband dies in a mysterious accident. The first book uncovers the truth behind his death and the following books in the series feature different mysteries for Alicia to solve along with Sneaky, the library cat and Fido, the golden retriever.

A Stone's Throw

myBook.to/Stonesthrow2

Between a Rock and a Hard Place **(Cobble Cove Mystery #2)**

myBook.to/CobbleCove2

Written in Stone

myBook.to/CC3ebook

Sneaky's Christmas Mystery (Cat Writer's Association Muse Medallion award-winning Cobble Cove story available in eBook only)

mybook.to/sneakyxmas

Sneaky's Summer Mystery (A Cobble Cove story in eBook only)

mybook.to/SneakySummer

Read an excerpt from Cobble Cove Mystery #5: *No Gravestone Unturned*

mybook.to/CobbleCove5

A Quarter to Midnight, Thursday, October 31, 2019, in the Cobble Cove Cemetery

Noah Burrows approached the cemetery gate. He fished in his pocket for the key and slipped it into the lock. It was nearly midnight on Halloween, and his father had instructed him to check the graveyard in case one of the local teens jumped the gate and messed up the tombstones with toilet paper as they'd done in the past. He was glad that the gate didn't creak open because he'd oiled it that morning.

Stepping through as quietly as his Adidas sneakers would allow, he spotted a figure in the back of the cemetery near the newly dug grave. It held a shovel and was digging at a nearby plot.

Trying not to alert the intruder, he avoided the leaves scattered around the grounds, but one crunched under his sneaker, and the masked man dropped the bag he was holding and turned to face Noah.

"Excuse me, but the cemetery is closed. If you don't leave now, I'll call the police." Noah removed his cell phone from his jeans pocket.

Before Noah could deflect the blow, the intruder raised his shovel and whacked the caretaker's son hard on the head. As the ground spun up to meet him and Noah fell across the grave the vandal was digging, the last thing he saw as things went black was the inscription on the stone: Kurt McKinney, beloved father of Gwendolyn, Kenneth, and John. (July 24, 1894 – September 3, 1964).

www.ingramcontent.com/pod-product-compliance
Lightning Source LLC
Chambersburg PA
CBHW051642260626
47170CB00004B/1286